The Case
⮜of the⮞
Case of
Kilcladdich

THE SIXTH ANTY BOISJOLY MYSTERY

The Case of the Case of Kilcladdich

CHAPTER ONE

Will a Still Still Still Still?

"My uncle couldn't meet you himself, Mister Boisjoly — he's blown himself up."

The popeyed son of the north face of Scotland who spoke these words of welcome was familiar to me — Ludovic MacAlistair was only and favoured nephew of Lummy MacAlistair, town patriarch, my intended host, legendary tipplemate of my late father, and master distiller of the legendary Glen Glennegie highland *eau de vie.*

"Oh, I say, that is unfortunate," I said with the distracted sympathy of a chap at the achy end of a lengthy journey by rail. "Not too serious, I hope."

"Difficult to say with any certainty," said Ludovic, his brow boughed, "until they've found all the bits."

A searching, North Sea wind swept across the creaking, Victorian-era railway platform and brought the gravity of the situation home to me, along with my charming travelling companion, Tiana 'Tannin' Tibbits, and my charming valet, Vickers.

"What bits?" asked Tannin.

"Lummy's blown himself up," I explained.

"Not really."

A fair point. I had only a distant recollection of young Ludovic, but that which I recalled was in the main a happy, high-minded half-wit. He hadn't changed appreciably — he shared with Tannin and myself a youthful late twenties, but he was elongated in a distinctly drainpipe motif, compared to my easily tailored trim and Tannin's concise but complex construction, inflating here and going in a bit there, as women tend to do. Byronesque, you might call Ludovic at a distance, and even moreso as you approached and saw that he favoured waistcoats of daring design in silk brocade, glittery watch chains, and riding boots.

"Are we quite sure of our facts, Ludos?" I asked. "I recall last time I was here, ten years ago to the day, you greeted us with the announcement of your pending marriage…"

"That was fleeting."

"…to a mermaid."

"Ah, yes…" Ludovic smiled vacantly at the melancholy memory of what might have been.

"You're quite sure that your uncle's been blown up?"

Ludovic turned his attention towards the town, and ours followed. The train station at which we had just arrived is five Scottish miles across stony flats and spongy marshes from the village of Kilcladdich, this side of the gorge of Glen Glennegie from its sister settlement of Kildrummy. A column of smoke stood still and significant at the centre of a scatter of stone houses and churches and pubs, reaching up past the expansive black backdrop of the North Sea, and into the colourless sky.

"Quite sure," concluded Ludovic.

"How's your aunt holding up?" asked Tannin, with reference to Molly MacAlistair, wife of the deceased.

"A woman of fond and fiery passions, kept very well in check." Ludovic looked sadly downward. "She had a quick one to his memory and then sent me to collect you."

"Should we even stay on?" wondered Tannin. "I would have thought there'd be a period of private grieving."

"Of course," agreed Ludovic. "But it's already been two hours and a bit. Do you want to have a wee look-in, on the way to the inn, Mister Boisjoly? It's probably something best experienced before dining."

"Call me Anty," I begged, as a mercy to the family sorrow, normally pronounced 'Bo-juh-lay', like the wine region, but in the pragmatic brogue of the northern reaches it just sounds angry as do, for instance, the words 'porridge' and 'cauliflower'. Anty,

2

an abbreviation of Anthony, is friendly on every tongue and hence pitches much closer to my famous disposition.

"I think I'll settle in at the inn, first, Ludovic, and let Vickers perform any necessary light maintenance," I said, and the proposition was unanimously approved. Ludovic loaded our bags into the back of the company barrel van and bounced us toward the column of smoke.

"Rummy thing, what, Vickers?" I said from the fireside chair of my stone and timber room above the Mash and Mashie, the best and worst inn in the dual villages of Kilcladdich and Kildrummy. Vickers had been unpacking my trunk but was struck stump still by some extraordinary feature of one of my suits.

"Most uncanny, indeed, sir," said Vickers. I knew immediately that we were in different time zones. It's not always clear, but when Vickers gets that haunted air about him it means that some sprocket has failed to engage. The man is a peerless gentleman's personal gentleman and has been so since Queen Victoria's wild youth, but it's back there and then that patchy portions of his perception still reside. "I appear to have packed three hunting suits."

"You did, Vickers — we're in Scotland, at Kilcladdich," I reminded him. "You felt that tweed was best suited to northern wind conditions."

"We're here for the tasting," recalled Vickers. You could hear the gears clicking into place.

"Exactly. I've been offered my father's seat on the jury to select which distillery gets to call itself Glen Glennegie."

"Has it been ten years already?" Vickers looked wistfully around the room.

"I know," I commiserated. "1919 seems like a fog-filtered yesterday, doesn't it? When Papa profited from our time here to pass from father to son the timeless tradition of falling off a pub roof into a peat bog."

3

"I often wonder what became of Eek Eric," mused Vickers.

"The Eriskay pony you seconded to pull us out?" I asked. "Last seen Papa was trying to ride him to Lochmaddy, with a view to giving him his freedom. Reparations had to be paid."

"Is this the rummy issue to which you refer, sir?"

"No, actually, I was speaking of the explosion."

"Oh, yes, of course, the explosion," recalled Vickers with a sustained squint. "Most unfortunate for Mister MacAlistair."

"Is it though?"

"I should think, at least from the perspective of his loved ones..."

"No, I mean to say, is it mere misfortune, or might someone have taken a hand?" I speculated. "Rather a coincidence, isn't it, this happening just before a tasting that will ensure the success of one distillery over another."

"It is precisely owing to this rivalry, sir, that the occurrence is most likely an accident," said Vickers, arranging my tweed suits by some criteria known only to him and, indeed, probably not even to him. "To guard the secrets of the process, the final stages of distillation of Kilcladdich and Kildrummy are performed by the master distiller, alone, in a room on the top floor of the respective distilling buildings, which is locked from the inside for the duration."

"Well, there you have it, practically got the Boisjoly brand right on the label," I said. "I'll first just topple down for the traditional inaugural tipple." I took up the flat cap that I wear when facing the north sea or playing rummy in a costermonger's pub. "Talking of which, Vickers, touching on the unspoken..."

Vickers checked me with a raised pair of argyle socks.

"Of course, sir." Vickers spoke in hushed tones. "As in your father's day, my lips are sealed."

"Good chap," I said and, much relieved, I took my leave.

The bar room of the Mash and Mashie is a damp, dark, draughty den smelling of whisky-steeped stavewood and tobacco, and ornamented with antique golf clubs nailed to the walls. In short, it was almost entirely like all pubs north of Glasgow, distinguished only by the presence of what must have been one of the few Tannin Tibbits for miles around.

"What ho, Tidbit," I called from the bar, where I had paused to negotiate a stoup of usquaebach and sourcewater. Tannin occupied a smooth-worn table formed of centuries of thick, black dock paint by a deep stone window of grey gloom. She raised a finger as I spoke, warning away future distractions, as she dribbled crystal river water into two fingers of whisky, like a fastidious poisoner taking pride in her trade. She had washed away the day's journey and changed from travel burlaps into pubbing tweeds, and folded her hair beneath a well-pinned shooting cap. She was still mostly girl when I had seen her first and previously, ten years ago, and still had a fresh-from-the-factory twinkle about her.

I sat across from Tannin as she completed the ritual and then just stared happily at the result, her chin in both hands, her apple cheeks dimpled with a dreamy smile.

"If you're too overcome, Tannin old thing, I can drink that for you," I offered.

"It'll be my first whisky at source in a year," she explained. "I'm savouring the moment." She took up her glass and trickled a taste down her throat. Then she held the elixir up to the light. "Have you noticed that in London, Anty, everything tastes just a bit like London?"

"The trick is careful pairing," I said. "I always privilege the strong portos when dining riverside, and stay clear of the oysters and ripened fowl at Claridge's when Oswald Mosely is in the house."

"What did you opt for?" asked Tannin, referring to my choice of local legend.

"Five year Kildrummy '06," I replied, holding my glass up such that it might be appraised at eye level.

"Ah," spoke Tannin with reverence. "The year of the controlled grass fires upstream at Baldibble."

"Exactly." I moved the glass gently under my nose. "Strains of sedge smoke and springtime. You?"

"Eight year Kilcladdich '19, as it happens." Tannin drew dreamily on her dram. "For nostalgia's sake."

Kilcladdich '19 is known outside of the immediate region as Glen Glennegie '19, for reasons which doubtless by now need a little explaining. Ten years prior to this eventful afternoon, Tannin's father, my father, and a wealthy virtuoso tippler named Mortimer Sheercliffe formed the jury which selected the distillation that would have the right to call itself Glen Glennegie for the next decade.

Tannin's father was principal distributor of the stuff, and Tannin inherited the business and the sacred vote. My father's seat on the jury was assured by his extraordinary gift for the subtle nuance, which I inherited, and because he was Glen Glennegie's second largest single customer, the first being the catering committee of the Royal Naval and Military Club. Tannin and I had learned of the discounted retirements of our respective fathers on the train coming up that morning.

"Seen anything of old Sheercliffe?" I asked.

"No," said Tannin, "and it's improbable we will, either, his clock stopped in '27 — decidedly late in life he took up mountain climbing and skydiving, the first leading inexorably but involuntarily to the second."

"Oh, right. Any idea who takes his place on the jury?"

"Not the haziest." Tannin shook her head distractedly. "He left no sons, so far as I know. Has a brother in Canada but the poor sap is in the maple syrup trade, so, there'll be none of that."

"No daughters?" I queried. "We live in a modern age and, after all, you're here."

"I'm exceptional, in every way." Tannin exalted in the atmosphere above her glass, making a spectacle of the fact that she, too, had the gift. "So was Mortimer."

"True," I agreed, and raised a glass in memory of Two-Fisted Sheercliffe. "His will be a big shot glass to fill — a man of discerning taste, a cultivated palate, and by all appearances a hollow leg."

"Hear hear."

"I look forward to welcoming what will doubtless be a giant among men to our pantheon." I finished my '06 and Tannin similarly disposed of her '19. "I am, I believe, sufficiently restored to discharge the promised wee look-in. Care to join me?"

"At the distillery explosion? Whatever for?"

"Oh, you know how these things go — sometimes what looks like a mundane explosion at a distillery can turn out to be something quite sinister," I explained. "It's rather in the way of being my area of special interest."

"What is? Distillery explosions?"

"Not exclusively, no," I said. "I'm often called upon to smooth some surprisingly stubborn societal seam. Perhaps you read of Cynthia Hannibal-Poole's New Year's Eve scavenger hunt across London?"

"Weren't the papers describing that as the scandal of the decade and the end of civilization as we know it?"

"Exactly," I confirmed. "Cynthia was particularly pleased with the headline in *The Times* which read, simply, 'Despair', in tombstone letters. You have no idea how disappointed she'd have been had I not been able to source two penguins and a submarine. At dashed short notice, too, even if it's me saying so."

"Still, seems rather a departure from suspicious explosions."

"It does, I agree," I agreed. "Closer to the issue to hand might be my contribution to the case the papers are calling The Tale of the Tenpenny Tontine, in which I sorted out how an apparent duel behind locked doors turned out to be murder."

"I thought that was a Scotland Yard chappie called Wittersham," reflected Tannin.

7

"Inspector Wittersham and I have a very creative dialectic, and he defers to me on many such matters," I said. "I strive to keep a low profile, you understand, the better to move freely about the metropolis."

Tannin turned to the window and gave careful consideration to the drizzle.

"I don't know that I'd be of much use, Anty," she said. "What do you say we focus on our respective strengths — if you'll take a good, hard look at the distillery, you see, I can stay here — or perhaps over there, by the fire — and concentrate on the distilled. Then, later, we can compare notes."

"Oh, right oh," I agreed.

"And someone should probably be here to welcome Sheercliffe's replacement when he arrives," added Tannin.

Kildrummy and Kilcladdich are both built along the same coastal road, divided by the generous Glen Glennegie river ravine, which supplies the icy clear hill water that balances the local magic. The villages occupy the northern nape of Britain and turn a cold, courageous face to the black, infinite sea beyond. Between the towns and the cliffy, craggy coast is a rangy, cracked, broken and racked golf course formed of roughs like quarries, water hazards deep and wide enough to have acquired their own monster myths, bunkers that have swallowed cattle, and eighteen uneven greens divided by a ravine.

Fog and rain played merrily together but welcomed a cold ocean wind when it pitched up and proposed slapping a frigid mist into my face as I walked the short distance from the pub to the smouldering distillery.

The cobbled street was slick with ambient damp and empty but for a puff of fluff of a lamb, tapping briskly towards me as though late for an appointment.

"What ho, woolly whelp." I tipped my hat as I passed, and the lamb skidded to a stop and gave me one of those glances I get quite often in London from people who think they know me but can't quite recall if they should admit to it. He held my gaze for longer than would be socially acceptable in the delicately nuanced conventions of the metropolis, but these small towns can be refreshingly uninhibited. I passed along without judgement. The lamb, thinking, presumably, that I must have known the way, fell into step behind me.

The distillery was a twin to the malt house. Both were squat, split rock and mortar blocks, two wide stories tall, and each had convex slanted roofs topped with a louvred chimney box that looked like a little brass pagoda. The ground floor was mostly one big furnace, with low barn doors through which peat moss fuel could be shovelled to taste. The distillery, I reasoned, was the one from which smoke billowed from the upper floor doorway. I clanked up the exterior, wrought-iron stairs.

A heavy, clammy cloud obscured the room, linty with specks and spots of floating debris. Crossing each other in the fog were grimy beams of light from the chimney and high, narrow vents between the roof and the top of the wall. The air was heavy with wood smoke, peat smoke, the steam and sulk of an extinguished fire, and four hundred years of distilled malt mash. The centre of the room — indeed, most of the surface the size of a hotel dining room — was an immense kettle, rising to the chimney in an increasingly complex composition of pipes and valves and bulbs and coils and pots, each with its own, vital role in the separation of ethanol (and its poisonous, highly incandescent, foul-minded cousin, methanol) from the fermented mash.

"Hark," came a word of wonder and awe from somewhere in the murk. "What stirs there in the mist? Can it be the spirit of my uncle with some message from the beyond?"

"Oh, what ho, Ludovic." I recognised the voice and, I remembered in the moment, the decidedly esoteric world view. "No, just Anty Boisjoly. No message."

"Hullo, Anty." Ludovic sailed out of the fog like an unsteady mast. "What brings you by?"

"You suggested it, Ludio," I reminded him. "Where's your uncle?"

"My uncle, Anty…" Ludovic folded his hands and lowered his eyes, "…my uncle has voyaged on to that undiscovered country, perchance to sleep, perchance to dream…"

"No, I mean, where are the remains?"

"Oh, right." Ludovic looked behind him, in the general direction of the other side of the kettle. "Mostly back there, but inventory is far from complete. It was a tremendous explosion — some fluke spark must have been introduced into the distilling room while Uncle Lummy was steaming off the methanol. We're just waiting on the mortician to come down from Baldibble."

"We?"

"Hmm?"

"You said 'we'. 'We're' just waiting on the mortician."

"Yes." Ludovic gazed once again at his hands. "Nasty business. In my cable I suggested that he bring a rake."

An otherworldly glow emerged from the other side of the kettle, illuminating a familiar face above a kerosene railway lamp.

"Ludio, what's taking you so... oh, hullo Anty." It was Isabette MacAngus, a dizzying redhead that I vividly recalled from my last visit to Glen Glennegie. Since then, if possible, her long lava hair had grown more viscous and her alabaster face more blue-eyed and becoming.

"What ho, Bettes," I hailed back. "Better circs, and all that, but delighted to see you again."

"Touching on that, Anty," said Ludovic, "I wonder if for the moment you wouldn't mention seeing Isabette here."

"Oh, right oh," I said, but without the conviction of the sentiment. "Oh, I say — your families aren't still feuding are they?"

"Worse than ever," replied Isabette. "Best if they didn't know that Ludovic and I are, you know…"

"Are you and Ludovic you know?"

Ludovic gazed at Isabette with the guileless devotion a basset hound reserves for an unattended slice of cottage pie. "Ours is a love fashioned by the fates, Anty, in the very same forges in which sunsets are hewn, laughter is loomed, where songbirds are tuned…"

"Yes, all right, less of that, Ludovic." Isabette moved idly toward a discreet turn around the kettle and Ludovic and I followed. "My uncle is determined to win back the Glen Glennegie label this year, Anty, and he'd cut off my entire branch of the family — past and future — if he knew that I so much as let a MacAlistair cross my field of vision without spitting."

"Uncle Lummy, for the record, held similar views with respect to the MacAngus family," reported Ludovic.

"So, you'll keep it all quiet, won't you Anty?" summed up Isabette.

"Keep what quiet?" Tannin appeared in the mist.

"That Isabette and I are in love," replied Ludio.

"Oh, right, well, congratulations."

"For pity's sake, Ludio," lamented Isabette.

"Ah, yes, of course," realised Ludovic. "Tannin, you must swear a blood oath to never breathe a word of what you have heard here today."

"Oh, uhm, right oh, Ludio," avowed Tannin. "If I'm completely honest, there's a good chance I'll have forgotten it by tea time."

"Forgotten what?" This time the intruder was another MacAngus — a striking Viking of a woman with sizzling red locks and the wily, wise allure of one who could only be Isabette's mother, Yvaine MacAngus, snappily sheathed in burgundy worsted wool. "And what are you doing here, Isabette MacAngus?" Yvaine cast a cold eye over Ludovic, who smiled guilelessly back.

"She was meeting me," I claimed quickly and, dare I say it, courageously. I recalled the chatelaine of Kildrummy with lucid, post-adolescent tremors formed of equal parts intimidation and admiration — a delicate poem of highland femininity, capable of pulling a wooden bung from a 19th-century barrel with her teeth. "I've long harboured fond memories of your enchanting daughter, Mrs MacAngus, and so on my return I arranged this discreet encounter."

Yvaine appraised me as so many mothers do, estimating the cut and cost of my tailoring with, judging by her curt but approving nod, uncanny accuracy. "Fair enough, but why would you arrange to meet my daughter at the scene of an industrial accident?"

"I'm an enthusiast."

"Of industrial accidents."

"Not just industrial accidents, no," I prevaricated. "I'm also a fond aficionado of the Piccadilly Circus bus breakdown and just *try* to keep me away from a double-booking at the Savoy."

"I remember you now," nodded Yvaine with grave surmise. "But you've got the wodge on tap, I recall."

"I have the sad but decidedly lucrative distinction of being my father's sole beneficiary, yes."

"Well, it's all to the good, then," declared Yvaine with all the maternal joy of a fishmonger unloading the last of the halibut. Yvaine had been a widow since before I first came to Glen Glennegie, and had since functioned as the pragmatic-minded MacAngus matriarch in spite of marrying into the family. Her late husband's brother, Duncan MacAngus, had always struck me as happy with the arrangement, so long as he was left to determine every detail in the distillation of Kildrummy.

"Spry thinking, Anty," said Isabette after her mother had sped off to see what she could get for this news on the always lively Glen Gennegie gossip market.

"Yes." Ludovic levelled a squint on me that he doubtless meant to express quiet menace, but came across more as a light hyperopia headache. "Quick work, Anty."

"Leave it out, Ludio," instructed Isabette. "Anty was magnificent, and our secret's safe."

"What's all this about secrets?" boomed the foghorn delivery of none other than the recently widowed Molly MacAlistair, a woman of strong views and sinews. She hove into the mist like a barge and bore down on me like a runaway barrel. I recalled and recoiled instantly, owing to a small misunderstanding that by then, certainly, she'd long forgiven and forgotten. "What's this drunken sot doing here?"

Molly MacAlistair figured in my recollections as an unknown and unknowable peril — like an angry snowman. She was constantly and consistently dressed in royal purple frocks that she'd been making herself from the same bolt of flannel since a container of drapery fell off a Dutch freighter and washed ashore in 1902. I figured in her recollections, I expect, in much the same way as does Prussia in Napoleon's memoirs.

"Hullo, Mrs MacAlistair. My condolences for your husband."

"The drink was bound to get him," she said, "one way or t'other."

"Maybe a trifle mawkish for the headstone," I said, "but a lovely sentiment nevertheless."

Molly, possibly for the best, had been ignoring me in favour of Isabette. "And what's a MacAngus doing in a MacAlistair distillery?"

"Oh, ehm, chaperoning me," said Tannin believing, possibly, that it was her turn to step up.

"Why?"

"Eh?"

"Why would you be needing a chaperone?"

"Oh, you know how people talk," she said. "I was meeting Ludio, you see, here in the distillery."

"The burning distillery."

"Yes, well, the fire's mainly out, now," said Tannin through the smoke. "Thought it might be romantic."

Molly took us all in with the jaundiced eye of the Bow Street magistrate within waving distance of his pension — the sort who knows that I and eight friends didn't really climb onto the pediment of the National Gallery to put a baby bird back in its nest, but has lost his zeal for the cut and thrust of the courtroom dialectic. She shook her head in despair for a wretched generation, and turned to go.

She paused at the door to peer back through the clearing smog and advise me, "Don't think I won't have my eye on you, Boisjoly." And she was gone.

"That went well, I think," adjudged Tannin.

"Shush." I put a finger to my lips. "I expect Isabette's uncle along momentarily.

"He's locked up in his own distillery," reported Isabette. "We won't see him for days."

"That still leaves the population of two entire villages — why is everyone stopping here, anyway?"

"On their way to the pub," explained Isabette with the tone of one pointing out the obvious answer to a simple-minded question. "Between the village and the pub there are almost no other distillery fires to draw the attention."

"Oh, say, that's right, Anty, it's why I've come, too," recalled Tannin. "You'll want to come back to the Mash and Mashie, straight away."

"Is Vickers dancing on the tables?" I asked. "I'll come, of course, because it's always a delight to see him happy, but there's little anyone can do to stop him. Best to just let it run its course."

"No, nothing like that," said Tannin. "In fact, I think your man is asleep on the chessboard."

"On reflection, that's an infinitely more likely state of affairs," I said. "Are his eyes open?"

"Not entirely."

"Is he speaking?"

"Reciting might be more accurate, if it's not being pedantic."

"Then it's impossible to say," I concluded. "Is that why you think I should return to the pub?"

"Not directly that, no," said Tannin. "It's rather what he's managing to sleep through that you ought to witness."

"You intrigue me strangely, Tidbit." I then bade farewell to the young lovers. "We'll leave you to your tryst."

"It's not a tryst, Anty," protested Isabette.

"It's a kind of tryst," corrected Ludovic.

"No, it isn't Ludio," insisted Isabette. "We're examining the scene of the accident."

"Are we?" asked Ludio.

"If anyone comes along and asks, yes, we're examining the scene of the accident." To demonstrate the point, Isabette raised her lamp and looked about in the now clearing fumes. "For instance, what do you lot make of that?"

"Of what?" some variation of which we all asked.

"That, right there." Isabette pointed to something which, now that it was brought to my attention, was quite conspicuous — all shredded red on grey ash.

"What is it?" I asked the general assemblage.

The general assemblage replied as one; "A spent flare."

CHAPTER TWO

A Twisty Misty Mystery of Distilleries and Whisky

Ludovic lingered in the mist and it was Isabette who was dispatched to the post office to cable the constabulary. Tannin and I walked back to the Mash and Mashie in contemplative silence, but for a clackity accompaniment on the road behind us.

"I say, Anty, are those sheep following us?" asked Tannin, gesturing discreetly with her shoulder at an entourage which had, indeed, grown to two. My earlier companion had been joined by another, smaller and, if possible, even more care-worn lamb. Both stopped when I did, and they met my eye with a hopeful, soulful, doleful gaze.

"They may just be heading to the pub," I speculated. "But I doubt it. The bigger one — the one who looks like he could be marginally less easily talked into an all-in round of Three Card Monty — followed me to the distillery."

"Perhaps they just like you."

"Goes without saying, Tanners," I confirmed. "And nothing would give me greater pleasure than to cavort with them — doubtless they know where the bright young things gather in Kilcladdich — but you spoke propitiously of jests and japes at the pub, I believe."

"It's rather in the way of something you need to see."

"It's not a rooster who can predict racing results, is it?" I asked. "Because I won't be falling for that a third time."

"Here we are…" Tannin pushed through the door of the Mash and Mashie and into the tumult.

It wasn't the standard pub tumult — the babble and bedlam that is the scientifically inevitable reaction of the judicious mix of locals, whisky, and seven o'clock — in fact the few scattered

16

ratepayers, including Yvaine MacAngus and Molly MacAlisatir, were cradling their whisky-and-waters in silent awe of the whirlwind who'd assumed centre stage.

"On the eighth hole I biffed it into the bunker — the one on the cliff with sand like the gravel they put under railroad tracks…" She was a broad, kettle-drum of a woman, dressed in golfing tweeds and speaking the fluent East End Pickpocket that everyone outside of London thinks of as the London accent. She posed with a niblick, or a mashie, or a brassie or, possibly, I don't know one golf club from another. "…so between me and the green is what amounts to a rampart — I'd have stood a better chance of breaking out of Borstal."

"You're right, Tannin old cannon," I said. "I wouldn't have missed this for tea at the palace."

"Wait…" Tannin checked me with a raised hand. "There's more."

"The wind's whipping over the cliff like the Flying Scotsman…" continued the tempest. "…so what did I do?" She positioned herself to reproduce her shot, and then turned on her heel. "Took my sand iron…" Sand iron! That would have been my next guess. "…and beat it right out to sea. Flew like a clay pigeon, out past the cliff, then stopped, hung in the air like a little round clot of cloud, and then the wind took it right back, over my head, and set it down gently on the green, a yard from the hole. One under bogey."

Light but sincere applause followed this dramatic reveal, and the narrator, Tannin and I formed a nexus at the bar.

"Is this the latest thing in Boisjolys, then?" she boomed at Tannin.

"Anty, Shelby Sheercliffe," presented Tannin. "Mortimer's widow, and the third chair of the Glen Glennegie jury."

"Oh, right oh," I said, as a neutral placeholder for, I think, 'blimey.'

"Not quite what you expected, eh Boisjoly?" asked Shelby.

"Not even close to what I expected," I confessed. "I thought that Mortimer was unmarried."

"He was, when you saw him last," confirmed Shelby. "We met on the links in Le Touquet in '21. Luck of the draw mixed amateurs open. It was love at first double under par."

"Couple's derby?" I asked.

"Elimination tourney," said Shelby. "I sent him to the clubhouse in the first round."

"I expect he appreciated that."

"He did," agreed Shelby. "He loved golf, but he loved whisky more. Perfectly reasonable matter of personal preference, on the links, a little less so when applied to mountain climbing, but we had a good six years. Whisky, thanks, landlord." This last sentiment was expressed to the white-whiskered map of cracks and crevices who appeared behind the bar. The landlord gazed flatly at her, as though not hearing because, in a very real way, he was deaf to the phraseology.

Tannin's bemused eyebrows expressed a clear, 'Eh? What do you make of that, then?'

"He needs to know what sort of whisky you want," I clarified in a discreet whisper.

"Doesn't matter," off-handed Shelby, much less discreetly and with an instant effect on the entire pub only slightly more dramatic than if she'd drawn a gun and shot someone. Silence fell upon the assembly like a wet tarp. Then Shelby made it worse. "Just any Scotch and soda."

"Ha!" covered Tannin. "Very droll, Shelby. She'll have the eight year Kilcladdich '12. So will I, I think. With river water."

The crinkly dial behind the bar grew more crinkly still. He reached up blindly to his right, took hold of an old church key suspended from a bell, and gave it a clang. Then he wandered idly off and presently was replaced by another relic who described quite similarly, except instead of whiskers he had a Father Christmas beard and instead of a thin clay pipe he smoked an oaken calabash.

"Two Kilcladdich '12, please, Angus," said Tannin, still bright with emergency bonhomie.

18

Angus MacAlistair was one of the two professional apportioners, bookending Alistair MacAngus and, if it's not belabouring the obvious, each represented the Kilcladdich and Kildrummy interests, respectively. To illustrate the point for the benefit of Shelby, when she and Tannin had received their whiskies and water, I asked for a ten year Kildrummy '16 (the year they traded a quarter of their casks with the Dunmorley Irish distillery). Angus repeated the ritual — he reached up, seized the church key, jangled it curtly, and stood aside, to be replaced by Alistair.

"Ten year Kildrummy '16, is it?" asked Alistair in that rhetorically pointless way of the best barkeeps. He pulled up a bottle and a glass but then stopped, held the glass up to the light, and said to Angus, "You call that clean, ya busted stave?"

"Ya pint and a half of pity," countered Angus. "You've all the memory of a bad morning of a good night — *you* cleaned that, doubtless to the very limits of your abilities."

"No, you dried cork, I didn't," claimed Alstair. "You know how I know I didn't? Because it still reeks to the clouds of that Kilcladdich swill, that's how I know." Alistair found another glass as he addressed me. "I'll just get you an uncontaminated tassie."

"So, you inherited your husband's place on the jury," summarised Tannin to Shelby.

"No." Shelby downed her straight whisky in a gulp and clapped her glass down on the bar. "Another one of whatever that was, landlord." Alistair coldly rang the bell, once again, and Angus popped up to fill the order, which Shelby took up. "No, I inherited my husband's coal mine, railway fitters, newspaper, thoroughbred stables, and a royal appointment for saddle polish. The seat on the jury, I expect, was a side-effect of all that." Shelby emphasised this proposal by raising her glass, in two separate lifts, to Yvaine MacAngus and Molly MacAlistair, each of whom returned the salute and drank in rhythm with Shelby but not, somehow, with each other.

"So much nicer by the fire, don't you think?" proposed Tannin with a conspiratorial eyebrow raised in my direction.

"Oh, rather," I agreed. "Particularly on a cold evening."

"You two petunias should try mountain climbing, then you'd know cold," suggested Shelby, but followed us nevertheless to the relative seclusion of three high-backed chairs by the fire.

"Would it be fair to say, Shelby," posed Tannin with an opening-of-proceedings tone, "that you're not really much of a connoisseur of whisky?"

"No, it would not be fair to say that," replied Shelby cooly. "Love the stuff." And she downed her share, once again, in a single gulp.

"Yes, indeed, that's very clear, no dispute there," effused Tannin. "It's just, you see, the duty of the jury is to select the absolute best and most consistently balanced distillation over the course of the previous decade since five years prior to the last time the jury convened — ten bottles, selected by the distiller and aged to his discretion, from 1915 to 1925."

"And it's vitally important to like the stuff, as you say," I continued, "and you've got that bit nailed down tight, but it's also dashed useful to have an appreciation of what we call the nuance, you see."

"You wouldn't be trying to patronise me, would you, Boisjoly?"

"Well, yes, obviously I'm patronising you, Shelby," I said. "But as you get to know me and, I hope, we become friends, you'll come to understand that I patronise everybody. It's very nearly a speech impediment. Nevertheless the point stands..." I held my glass up so that the liquid might filter the light of the fire. "...there are four hundred years of tradition in this imperial gill of amber enchantment. Artisans have refined and improved the process over a lifetime at the end of which they've laid down barrels that they knew would only ever be enjoyed by a new generation of patronising palates." I lowered my voice to a wary, war-time whisper. "Neat, or with a little river water or rainwater and never, ever, above all not within a hundred miles of Glen Glennegie, with soda."

"Pish."

"You may well say 'pish'," I conceded. "Or 'pshaw' or even 'tch', but that doesn't alter your weighty responsibility as a member of the Glen Glennegie jury to select the very best distillery to represent the name."

"They're all just wobble water."

"Yes they are," I agreed. "But each wobble has its own potential and personality and pedigree, a pedigree that begins with fastidious selection of the barley..."

"...which is then malted," continued Tannin, speaking in reverent tones, "meaning it's allowed to begin germination, and then that process is halted at a very precise moment, in the heat and smoke from smouldering peat which, itself, has been carefully collected and curated."

"What is peat moss, anyway?" asked the philistine, with a promising curiosity.

"It's decaying plant matter, typically from a bog," explained Tannin, with a touching, affectionate inflexion that elevated decaying plant matter to something near ambrosia, particularly when sourced from a bog. "In its dried form it makes excellent fuel and it imparts an earnest, earthy subtlety to malt, which makes itself known, in its own time, in the future final product."

"This malted barley is then milled into a mash, which is then reduced to a slurry with the fanciful name of 'wort'," I said. "It's formed of the sugars — alchemied into existence by some organic magic during the aforementioned germination process — and the timeless waters of Glen Glennegie."

"To this is added a hand-reared, living yeast, which initiates the fermentation process." Tannin's eyes dazzled and her voice trilled with child-like wonder.

"The sugars are now converted to alcohol by yet another mystical method for which we are all thankful," I said, "and in due course the wort is ready for distillation."

"It's not done yet?"

"Oh, no," differed Tannin. "Now it becomes a precise and yet highly subjective science — in the distilling house, an entirely new source of heat is slowly raised beneath the ferment to separate the head, the heart, and the tail."

"Methanol, ethanol, and lees, which evaporate at progressively higher temperatures," I clarified. "But it's down to the distiller to decide precisely when to make this consequential distinction, which can leave ethereal traces in the heart."

"And that's the nuance you two are going on about," supposed Shelby, incorrectly.

"Barely the beginning," amended Tannin. "The next step is the most important in the entire life cycle of the elixir — now the distillate retires to quietly commune with past masters and distant cousins." In the absence of a gilded pedestal, Tannin held her glass above us and spoke now in hushed, awed tones. "For no less than three years and often as many as sixteen, it sleeps in centuries-old oak — wizened barrels from Glen Glennegies of centuries past, cuves from Cognac, Spanish casks that have hosted generations of Sherry, even sour mash kegs from America — these elders cultivate, educate, ripen, and refine the young innocent into, with patience and appreciation... whisky."

"This is why we like to specify, when we select our point of engagement with the history of whisky, the label, year, and the age, which is the time it spent in the barrel," I elucidated.

Shelby nodded abstractly and gazed at some epiphany in the middle distance. "I see." She handed her glass to Tannin. "Get me another one of these, will you?"

"Certainly, Shelby," said Tannin, with a tone of parental pride, like a mother whose child's first steps had been a simple but competent soft-shoe act. "Which one would you like to try?"

"Doesn't matter."

Tannin's maternal smile froze in that way that makes smiles mean something else entirely, as though her child's first steps, while at first promising, had devolved into dancing on the grave of a beloved ancestor.

"Shelby..." I leaned forward while Tannin went to the bar to get it matters not what. "Purely out of curiosity — don't know what makes me think of it — why did you accept the position on the jury?"

She had a ready and surprising reply. "The links."

"The golf course?"

"That's right," confirmed Shelby. "Morty always said it was the most challenging he's ever played."

When people lie to me, I find, it's a very effective tactic to say nothing for a bit, and just watch, expressionless, knowing, and wise.

"Why are you grinning like a half-wit who's been hit in the back of the head by a long drive?" asked Shelby flatly.

"You hardly need to sit on the Glen Glennegie jury to use the golf course."

"No, you're right," admitted Shelby. She looked into the fire and assumed a softer countenance, and I fancied that I could see what a younger, vulnerable Shelby might have looked like before she was bitten by a vampire. "You know, when you love someone, and you lose him, you're apt to get a little nostalgic... thanks, Tibbits..." Tannin returned with a resigned demeanour and handed over Shelby's refresher. "...I wanted to do something for Kildrummy and Kilcladdich. Leave a mark. A deep one."

"Talking of which," I veered sharply, "do you recall where you were when the explosion occurred?"

"You mean two hours ago when there was a ruddy great boom?" asked Shelby. "Yes, I think I can cast my back to that occasion. I was just teeing off for the sixth."

"What did you see?"

"Nothing but sky," answered Shelby, nostalgically. "I think the sudden boom might have helped — caught me off guard and I swiped the egg like it was an angry python. Two hundred yards if it was an inch."

"I mean, with respect to the explosion."

"Oh, that. The distillery blew up."

"Did you see anyone near the building?"

"Those two artefacts behind the bar." Shelby gestured with her chin toward Angus MacAlistair and Alistair MacAngus. "They've got more pep than you'd think, looking at them."

"They'd almost have to, wouldn't they?" noted Tannin, casting a discerning eye over the codgers, in that moment

23

apparently having a lively debate about which side of a beer map was up. I took leave and went to offer arbitration.

"What ho, tipple-twins." I leaned jovially on the bar and was assiduously ignored, as the subject under advisement had shifted to some finer point of the hospitality industry.

"Ach, ya wee bit a' used tat," reasoned Alistair. "You've all the sense the good lord gave a footprint."

"Ya dried spit of chewed mutton, ya," pointed out Angus. "You're as useful as a leather hammer, you are."

"Perhaps just the six year Kilcladdich '14," I endeavoured to divert, "with a splash of rainwater."

Alistair gave me just enough attention to say, "Just a wee moment, if you please sir," before resuming the exchange of ideas with Angus, "Ya poor drowned fish, perhaps the next time you've a task beyond your limits, buckling a shoe for a child, for example, or making change for a shilling paid on the price of a shilling, you'll let me know and stand your distance, so there's a chance it'll be with done the fewest number of fatalities."

With that calm counterpoint, Alistair seized the church key and gave the bell a clear and conclusive clang. Angus stepped up.

"Six year '14, you say, sir."

"Please."

"With a splash of rainwater, if I understand you correctly."

"If it's not too much bother."

"Can't be done, I'm afraid." Angus spoke with a resigned despair somewhere between fatalistic and apocalyptic.

"Oh, right." I reflected for a moment. "The eight year '12 then, I think. It seems to have inspired Miss Tibbits to new heights of hyperbole."

"Can't do that either, sadly," eulogised Angus. "Look here…" He drew a stoup from a clay cask and presented it to me. "…some mossy-headed mother's regret dropped his stinking great pipe into the rain barrel, as you can see."

And, indeed, the ladle was full of decidedly sooty water.

"My fault," confessed Alistair. "I lowered my guard long enough for this cross-eyed perplexion to empty the fireplace sweepings into what he doubtless thought, in his mollusc apprehension of this complex world, was the ash can." Here Alistair switched to a stage whisper. "Rain barrels and ash cans are quite similar, to be fair, if you've the reasoning of a bantling midge."

"How about a dash of source?" I proposed.

"Ah, now, that I can do, sir," said Angus with cautious optimism. "That is, unless the Abbot of Unreason has elected to discharge his duties, as he sees them, and done the washing up in the store of river water... Oh, you're in luck, sir, he hasn't got 'round to it yet."

"Cheers." I mixed my whisky and whisper and took a much needed taste. "I understand that you were witness to the explosion earlier today?"

"Aye," confirmed Angus. "The pub being empty, we were outside, enjoying the unusually fine weather."

We were distracted in that moment as a seagull was dashed against the window by the wind.

"A hearty south-easterly," observed Alistair.

"South-westerly," differed Angus. "We chanced to be watching the distillery when it happened, at precisely two-fifteen."

"Two-twenty," corrected Alistair.

"And why were you watching the distillery at that very moment?"

"Not much else to carry the attention, if I'm being honest," explained Angus. "And it was just as Lummy finished cooking off the head."

"You could tell that by looking?"

"You can know by the smoke," claimed Alistair.

"Unless you're a man of experience," said Angus. "Then you can tell just by the whiff."

"Did you see anyone near the building?" I asked. "Anyone with, say, a flare gun?"

"Not a soul," said Alistair, and Angus, reluctantly, agreed.

"But you couldn't see the other side of the building," I pointed out.

"Aye, we could," said Angus. "From the distillery to the gorge there's just the links."

"We'd have seen anyone as we ran over... unless he jumped off the ravine," added Alistair.

"So, what you're saying, gentleman," I surmised, "is that what we have here is a locked room mystery."

"No, we're not saying that," said Alistair.

"Oh, aye, we are," differed Angus, naturally.

CHAPTER THREE

The Meaning of the Memory of Molly and the Minister

"It's never a locked room mystery," contended Alistair. He then paused and appeared to weigh his words before adding, "Ya daft draught."

"The room was locked," argued Angus.

"Aye, the door was locked," conceded Alistair. "Most of us don't regard the locking of doors as so very mystifying as all that, but I understand if you need the notion explained in simple terms — Lummy MacAlistair barred the door from the inside, as he does whenever he's doing his distilling."

"Which, if you can navigate from that fact all the way to a second one without losing your way, is what renders the explosion a mystery. Put these two facts together — a locked room and a mystery, what have you got?" Angus said then, as an aside to me, "Please don't help him, Mister Boisjoly — he'll get there on his own, in time, and it does a heart good to see his simple joy when he works things out on his own."

"There's no mystery in that, either," protested Alistair. "He blew himself up."

Angus slowly shook his head, sadly, as one resigning himself to a lost cause.

"What this poor head of tangled yarn hasn't learned, even after years in the trade, is that stills are air-tight, and there's no risk of explosion."

"He was probably gagging for a drink," speculated Alistair.

"No one drinks straight ethanol," contended Angus.

"Oh, I don't know, might be an improvement over Kilcladdich." Alistair elaborated on this thought in an aside to me, "It's not a bad whisky, for what it is — it has a certain raw, unaffected charm, much like American moonshine or surgical antiseptic."

"Lummy didn't drink while he was distilling," insisted Angus. "Owing to rare, unfortunate historical events, he avoided the drink like the pox while he worked, and always kept a bottle of Kildrummy on hand, as a reminder how bad things can get." Angus directed further explanation to me, "Kildrummy is an excellent medicinal, you understand, and has been known to deter the most committed dipsomaniac."

"Lummy didn't drink while distilling," corrected Alistair, "owing to frequent, habitual incidents, such as, in no particular order, defending Moan Innes from an invasion of ill-intentioned kelpies — 'the luminous kind', to hear him tell it — armed with a wooden cleek, and somehow contriving to mislay an entire dray of peat moss, wagon and all, a puzzler which remains unsolved to this day."

"And yet…" pondered Angus, "…poor Lummy could hold his liquor like a marble statue of Walter Scott, compared to Duncan MacAngus whose attempt to toss a makeshift caber over Glen Glennegie gorge interrupted telegraph transmissions from Inverness to Aberdeen for a term of several weeks."

In the form of another aside for the benefit of the Boisjolys present, Angus added, "In the interests of public safety, Duncan MacAngus is currently sequestered in his own distillery," speaking the word 'distillery' as though it was a euphemism for 'mad scientist's laboratory'.

I have a keen ear for these things, and I began to sense conversation turning toward the adversarial. I endeavoured to steer us onto more topical ground.

"I say, in light of everything, do you expect we'll be proceeding with the tasting?"

"Why not?" asked Angus. Alistair, unable to find an objection to that view, said nothing.

"Death of one of the principal participants?" I suggested. "These things, suspicious or otherwise, often warrant a period of memorial observance."

"Best memorial to Lummy will be winning the Glen Glennegie label for the third consecutive decade," pronounced Angus. "And he's already chosen his ten bottles." Angus substantiated this claim with a nod towards a glass display cabinet, built into a pillar between the bar and ceiling of the pub. Behind the glass were two shelves, each with a little brass plaque. The top shelf read 'Kilcladdich', and the bottom shelf 'Kildrummy'. The Kilcladdich shelf supported ten bottles. The bottles had no labels, as such, just tags on their necks with handwritten names, dates, and ages, from 'Kilcladdich 1915, 6 years' to 'Kilcladdich 1925, 4 years'. The Kildrummy shelf was empty.

"I note there's yet no entry for Kildrummy," I observed.

"No," confirmed Angus. "The MacAngus mob have a very involved selection process, the unfortunate consequence of which is that the next day no one remembers what happened with any clarity. It may be a while yet."

"Duncan selects the Kildrummy entries personally," countered Alistair. "You see, Mister Boisjoly, unlike Kilcladdich, there are subtle and important differences between one year and another."

"Aye," acknowledged Angus. "The '05, as an example, had almost no reported cases of blindness."

"Why, Mister Boisjoly…" A kindly, syrupy, dangerously amiable voice approached from my blind spot. "…I didn't see you over here — Alistair, make sure that Mister Boisjoly's drinks are on the MacAngus cuff, won't you?"

Yvaine MacAngus' radish-red mane appeared at my shoulder and she placed her drink next to mine.

"Against the rules, Mrs MacAngus," I reminded her. "I'm on the jury, you see."

"You are?" Yvaine's talent for stagecraft was on a par with my own when, at the age of six, I portrayed Argan in *La Maladie Imaginaire,* and the broadly-held consensus, formalised in my end-of-year report and the Kensington News, was that the malady was more convincing. "I had no idea. A most excellent addition to the pantheon, if you don't mind my saying so."

"Oh, no, not at all, Mrs MacAngus," I assured her. "We Boisjolys are made of stern stuff."

"I was sorry to hear about your father."

"Me too," I commiserated. "He was the only one I had."

"I don't mind admitting, Anty, that I was pleased to know that you still held some trace of fondness for Isabette. Young people are rarely, in my experience, so consistent in their affections."

It may not seem that way, seeing it just written out flat like that, without the hills and valleys of melodrama, but that was top-quality twaddle. I may have made vague reference to it earlier, but Yvaine's affection for me hasn't been all so terribly consistent either. There was once a time, in fact, when she referred to me as 'a net negative'. That time, to be precise, was four o'clock in the wee hours, ten years ago.

My fondness for her daughter, back then, was measurably more than a trace, and after an evening, spilling into a night, of dispassionate reflection, I realised that it would be rash to not seize the moment and serenade the girl under her window.

The first obstacle I encountered was that the only piano — my accompaniment of choice — was in the church and, I reasoned, about as heavy as a piano. The second and only alternative was a bagpipe nailed to a beam at the Mash and Mashie. It's uncanny and illuminating how time can provide perspective and now, ten years later, I have no difficulty admitting that I have little talent for the bagpipe. I assumed, at the time, that the skillset was similar to that which is required for the penny whistle — a weapon for which I'd shown some aptitude in my youth — but in fact playing the bagpipes is much less like playing a tin flute than it is like effecting a citizen's arrest on an octopus that has cause to believe it's in the right.

The second problem was rather a two-parter — I didn't know which window was Isabette's and (this is part two) I thought I did. The result, if it's not obvious now, is that I woke Yvaine MacAngus at four o'clock in the morning with an admittedly sub-par rendition of *When A Fellow's On The Level With A Girl That's On The Square,* performed beneath her window. Relations, since then, had remained distantly cordial.

Now, though, the intervening period, during which I grew to man's estate and inherited my father's money and seat on the Glen Glennegie jury, had given Yvaine MacAngus time to re-evaluate her estimation of me. I elected to leverage this new dynamic with a subtle, probing enquiry.

"You didn't blow up Lummy, did you?"

"Of course I didn't blow up Lummy," answered Yvaine, with a quick return to old form. "I thought it was an accident."

"Do you recall where you were when it happened?"

Yvaine nodded. "At the Kildrummy distillery."

"I thought it was locked from the inside for the duration."

"T'is," confirmed Yvaine. "I wasn't *in* the distillery, I was *at* the distillery, outside, shouting in."

"Duncan stays locked up for the entire duration then, no exceptions."

"Not for food nor drink. Particularly not drink."

"All in aid of protecting the trade secret."

"Aye." Yvaine nodded and took another taste of whisky. "Lummy didn't trust Duncan, and Duncan didn't trust Lummy and, by extension, any of the members of either family. So they lock themselves in while they're doing the final distillation."

"Is there much to keep secret?" I asked. "I thought the process was mostly dictated by largely immutable laws of physics."

"Of course not," scoffed Yvaine. "Lummy MacAlistair locked himself in his distillery because Duncan MacAngus locked himself in his, and vice-versa. The malting and the ageing is all that matters when you're making whisky."

"May I ask what it was that you were yelling through the door of the distillery?"

"That." Yvaine gestured with her glass towards the cabinet. "I was reminding him that he had yet to select ten bottles of Kildrummy for the tasting."

"Is that unusual?"

"It's mighty close work, at any rate," opined Yvaine. "The tasting is on Friday and, according to the rules, if a candidate case isn't delivered by six o'clock on the day, it's disqualified."

"Can you not just take the decision on his behalf?"

Again, Yvaine shook her head. "He won't have it. He's got the case in there with him, the dark-hearted soak." Yvaine finished her drink in an appreciative swallow, and put her glass on the bar. "I hope you'll come and see us in Kildrummy, anytime you like."

And with that complete and avaricious policy shift, Yvaine left the pub, presumably to continue her important haranguing duties at the door of the Kildrummy distillery.

"Oh, what ho, Mrs MacAlistair," I said, for Molly MacAlistair had steamed over to the bar the moment that Yvaine's colours dipped below the horizon.

"Call me Molly." She demurely waved a kerchief of flannel most mauve.

"I will, with the occasional Boisjoly spin, if that's all right, Molls. You should call me Anty, by way of retaliation."

"I saw you talking to Yvaine MacAngus," observed Molly, casually, as though endeavouring through the art of casual conversation to catch out a Bosch spy.

"You did," I agreed. "Lovely woman. Very broad-minded in her appreciation of show tunes."

"What did she have to say?"

"Oh, I think it was rather in the order of a diplomatic function," I speculated. "I believe that she somehow discovered that I'm on the Glen Glennegie jury."

"Are you now?" Molly expressed her surprise at this news with a sincerity that made Yvaine's synthetic sincerity sound like the guileless declaration of affection between a boy and his dog. "I'm very happy to know it — you have your father's refined sensibilities, with perhaps fewer of his, ehm…"

"Excesses?" I suggested. "In all modesty, I agree. His was a cultivated and discerning palate, but his final word was suspect and, occasionally, incomprehensible, owing to an inability to drink less than an imperial pint in a single sitting."

"Lummy was very fond of him," reminisced Molly.

"They were jolly good friends," I recalled. This was more true than she knew, for the brief visits that my father made to Kilcladdich were, for Lummy MacAlistair, periods of boundless bounty and adolescent abandon. Molly's affection for her late husband was so deep and abiding that she obliged him to live within a set of protective guidelines that many might consider cloying, and that Lummy, by the testimony of my own ears, thought of as 'straight asphyxiation'. She disapproved of him gambling, smoking, drinking to excess or at all during daylight hours, swearing, tolerating swearing in others, spitting, and telling that one about the time Molly took the new young vicar for the doctor, coming to have a look at her sacroiliac.

My father was a man of very specific and targeted talents. He was a spectacular failure as an intelligence officer and his short-lived political career definitively and single-handedly interred the fledgling Kensington and Chelsea Secessionist Party. But his easy, almost instinctual knack for drinking around a given set of rules was properly uncanny. He brought this faculty with him when we went to Kilcladdich, and applied it generously to the problem of Lummy's incarceration. The strategy was cunning in its simplicity.

It amounted to this — I was always on hand and constantly at the ready, like a veteran hunting beagle, to respond to my father's sixth sense for the moment that Molly would inevitably turn up — sometimes with a military stealth that I once fancied she'd acquired in a secret youth, murdering pashas in their sleep — to check on her husband. I would snap into action and take up his cigar or cards or whisky, and he would produce my father's ironic, constant companion, *The Boy's Book of Moral Lessons from the New Testament,* and appear to be giving me a right good talking to.

I quite liked having a pivotal role in the whole operation, and it only ever put me at odds with Molly in any direct way when we were all pinched for the unauthorised construction of a toll booth on Glen Glennegie bridge. I had to claim that it was I who had told it to him when the constable — in open court and to broad audience approval — repeated the story of Molly and the new vicar.

"Do you recall where you were when the distillery exploded?" I asked.

"Malt house." Molly gave a nod towards the front of the pub through which, if it hadn't been there, we'd have been able to see the malt house. It's just this side of the distillery.

"What do you suppose happened?"

"Hard to say, with any certainty, but distillery explosions are hardly a discredited folk tale, are they?"

"So, you think it was an accident."

"I confess, I don't see how it could be." Molly shook her head sadly at the stubbornly opaque front of the pub. "The still was in good nick. Lummy was always dead careful."

"It couldn't have been some unanticipated consequence of this top-secret new process that he was hiding behind locked doors, could it?"

"There was never any secret process."

"Really?" I gaped. "I find that most extraordinary."

"Why?"

"Because that's what Yvaine thinks, too," I said. "She thinks that Duncan and Lummy were escalating an increasingly complex series of exercises in psychological warfare."

"I suppose you could call it that," mused Molly.

"What would you call it?"

"Being daft," she said with a flat, matter-of-fact judgement. "Lummy was sure that Duncan had no secret, and that he was locking himself in during the distilling just to make it look like he had, so Lummy locked himself in, too, to make it look like he really did have a secret."

"You mean to say that both men knew that the other was bluffing," I marvelled, "but they did it anyway?"

"I didn't object," said Molly, with misty-eyed nostalgia. "At least I knew where he was. Now I guess I always will."

We drank in silent memorial for a moment.

"I understand, in spite of everything, that we'll be proceeding with the jury."

"Aye," said Molly. "We can hardly deny Lummy his final victory, just because he's dead."

"That's what Angus said. Has Kilcladdich had a good decade?"

"It's a snip." Molly demonstrated the point with a luxurious draw on her whisky. "Whether or not Duncan delivers his case by the day after tomorrow." She nodded meaningfully towards the case of cases.

"Yes, Yvaine's concerned about that," I agreed. "Seems that Duncan's got the MacAngus case in the distillery with him, and she tells me that if he doesn't produce it soon it's an automatic disqualification."

"Those are the rules, handed down over the generations."

"Doubtless all based on sound, dispassionate reasoning." I pondered this, aided in the act by a sip of ponder-water. "Out of curiosity, what do the rules say should happen should neither case be delivered?"

"Then neither distillery has the right to use the name Glen Glennegie."

"You mean, it just ceases to be a label?"

"Aye." Molly finished her drink. "That'd be the end of Glen Glennegie."

CHAPTER FOUR

Of Muddy Tracks
and Sandy Traps
and Hereditary Handicaps

The afternoon had mutated, in that sudden, comprehensive way common to maritime climates, from drab grey to grey drab. I was retracing the steps of Angus MacAlistair and Alistair MacAngus to determine what could or could not be hidden from view between the distillery and the gorge when I had the eerie, subtle sense that I was being followed, an inkling given substance by the sound of clickety hooves.

My entourage of hopeful, skittish sheep had grown and now numbered five, mainly lambs, but also including a yellowing presbyter type, with a nevertheless trusting, guileless air about him. When I stopped and turned to look at them, the cortege, too, stopped and looked back up the street, to see what had drawn my attention. Satisfied that we weren't being followed, we continued on our way.

The geological survey was accurate as reported — between the pub and the distillery there was no place to hide, apart from the other side of the building, bordered by the gorge. I looked towards what I guessed was the sixth green and took note of two points of interest — Shelby would have seen anyone on the opposite side of the distillery, and Vickers was stuck in the mud. I pursued him across the tundra followed, like a wildly successful Bopeep, by an embarrassment of sheep.

"What ho, Vickers," I called from the edge of the tee-off ground — an island of green in a moat of mud. "I hope you're wearing your spats, by which I mean, of course, I hope you're not wearing mine."

Vickers looked down at his completely submerged feet.

"I'm unsure," he judged. "I shall endeavour to update you as soon as new information comes available. Will that be all, sir?"

"Unless you'd like to discuss your current predicament."

Vickers gazed towards the Mash and Mashie, and then slowly turned his attention back to me, scanning the links for clues along the way.

"I believe that I was looking for you, sir," he concluded at last. "You're not golfing, are you?"

"No, not golfing," I assured him. "I've always avoided the pastime, since my father first warned me off it — he said that I would be a poor golfer, owing to a congenital predisposition among the Boisjoly men to become easily bored. Why do you ask?"

"I feel that whatever drew me here was in some way related to golf."

"Well, it's a starting point," I said. "What makes you think so?"

"My pocket appears to be full of golf balls."

"Sound hypothesis, then. Any idea why?"

"Nothing concrete, for the moment, sir."

"Right, well, keep me posted," I urged. "In the meantime..." I found a narrow bit of moat and hopped over. "...let us apply a little creative landscaping to your situation."

Over the course of several heaping handfuls of sand from the tee box, I formed a small but serviceable peninsula. In moments, Vickers was once again above-ground.

"Thank you, sir."

"My noble obligation and personal pleasure, Vickers," I said. "And, as it happens, I was just now thinking how useful it might be to access the archives."

Vickers, if it needs be said, can be occasionally indifferent to current minutiae, such as where and when we are and whether or not tea can be made with gin, but he once hoarded matter and fact assiduously, right up until the coronation of George V, when he gave up the practice entirely.

Vickers and I proceeded along the coastal links toward the river. The sheep fell in line behind us. I provided the colour commentary. "Have you any recollection, Vickers, of mention of a secret, noncanonical distillation process employed by either Kildrummy or Kilcladdich?"

"Oh, yes, sir," said Vickers with concrete conviction. "It was commonly understood that prior to the match, the process was known and employed by both distilleries and, perhaps notably, it was not at the time regarded as a secret."

"Match? What match?"

"A golf game," elucidated Vickers. "Played between nominated champions of the MacAngus and MacAlistair families respectively, in 1767."

"Odd that a single golf match should become such an historical milestone."

"Not in the greater context, sir," differed Vickers. "The result of the game and subsequent accusations of cheating resulted in a rift between the families which has survived to this day. Perhaps you've noticed a certain animosity between the two camps."

"I have. Like the Capulets and the Montagues, played out against the jolly, back-slapping ambience of Macbeth."

"A most apt analogy, sir."

"So who won this mythic matchup?"

"Nobody remembers."

"Not really."

"Or at any rate, there's little agreement on the question," clarified Vickers. "The only point of common accord between the families is that the other side won by bold and determined deception."

"Just a tick, Vickers," I said. "Something doesn't quite add up — it's my peripheral understanding that people have been cheating at golf since the game was invented as, if my sources are correct, a method for clearing the snakes from the meadows of St Andrews. Among its proudest traditions, in fact, is the shaved scorecard, and hardly the sort of practice that sparks an enmity measured in generations."

"No, sir, the endurance of the animus is due to the stakes for which the game was played," said Vickers. "A division of resources which remains in force to this day, serving as a constant reminder of the wrong that each family feels was done to it by the other."

"Resources? What resources? There's nothing but the river and a network of peat bogs, cunningly distributed to trap even the most sober Londoner, so you can imagine what little chance *I* had."

"Precisely, sir," agreed Vickers. "The only remaining necessities in the manufacture of whisky are grain, which is sourced from surrounding farming villages, and casks, which are traded on distant and often international markets. The match was played for first access to the upstream waters of the river Glennegie, and to the peat moss."

"But, there's loads of peat moss. And it's self-perpetuating. As for the river, it's looking as bankish as ever. If anything, it's put on weight since I last saw it."

"The proximity that both villages have to peat bogs and the river, without either exercising direct municipal control, resulted in something of a race of attrition — each side moved further upstream to collect their water, and each would harvest their peat moss earlier and earlier in the season."

"I see," I twigged. "Like Storks and Harron."

"Yes, sir, a most helpful comparison."

"You've never heard of them."

"Ah." Vickers spoke with audible relief. "Then perhaps you would..."

"Just gearing up to it," I assured him. "Storks and Harron are members of my club. Both bachelors and the best of mates, right up until the smash premier of *Clowns in Clover* at the Adelphi. Have you seen it?"

"I believe not."

"You might not recall if you had," I said. "Not bad, as such, but almost deliberately forgettable. Like the ceiling of a dentist's office. The lead, however, was the undeniably delightful Esmée

Knotty-Nature — note, Vickers, that either that is a stage name or I've got it wrong or both, but the story holds up magnificently either way. Of course, Storks and Harron both fell for Esmée like tightly synchronised bags of coal."

"I'm not sure that I readily see the pertinence..."

"Not yet, no, it's an involved parable. You see, neither Storks nor Harron are what anyone would confuse with a lothario. Unpracticed, you might say, in the delicate art of seduction. They both had the equally unoriginal idea of lingering at the stage door every night with a bouquet of flowers."

"An expensive plan of approach."

"At any time, and this was during the carnation crisis of '27," I recalled. "Dark, dark times. Furthermore, the only competitive advancement on this strategy that either of these tragic manics could imagine was increasingly larger bouquets. I once looked in on them after a performance of *Blue Skies* at the Vaudeville — the alley looked like the funeral of a beloved racehorse."

"I begin to see the pertinence," said Vickers.

"Exactly," I confirmed. "They were putting each other into penury without either one improving his odds with the lovely Esmée."

"Was some sort of accommodation eventually reached?"

"In a manner of speaking," I said. "Closing night, Esmée broke the news to poor Storks and Harron — she was already married."

"Could she not have told them this sooner?" asked Vickers, heroically aggrieved on behalf of my clubmates.

"She could have done," I acknowledged. "But her first loyalties were to her husband, who owned the florist across the street from the theatre. The couple retired to the south of France that same year."

"Regrettably, no such externally imposed solution existed to settle the dispute between the MacAngus and MacAlistair families," said Vickers, "and so... sir, I'm convinced that those sheep are following us."

40

We had stopped at the edge of the river. Below us the currents rippled around Moan Innes, a peaty little island varying distances from either bank. Behind us, the sheep, believing that I had led them to this promised land, were grazing. They had also acquired reinforcements along the way, and I now boasted ten or eleven woolly acolytes.

"They're not following us, Vickers," I said. "They're following me. I suspect they've had some sort of breakdown in their ruling hierarchy, resulting in a power vacuum and thrusting me, for want of a more deserving leader, into political life. Same thing happened with Stalin. I shall look to you for frank counsel during my administration."

"Very good, sir."

"You were about to recount the riveting conclusion to the tale of the golf match — always a favourite theme of the great dramatists."

"Yes, sir," continued Vickers. "The objective was to eliminate the destructive competition for resources, and so the winner of the match would select for his family either preferential upstream access to the river waters, or first harvest rights of the peat moss season. The loser would claim the remainder."

"Then, surely we know who won the match."

"On the contrary," said Vickers. "Each side feels shortchanged. It's assumed by the MacAngus faction that the MacAlistairs cheated to gain control of the peat moss, while the MacAlistairs hold the view that it's the headwaters of the Glennegie which were the true prize."

"Why don't they just swap?"

"Apparently such an initiative was attempted, on several occasions, most recently as 1899, with mediation provided by the Reverend Emeritus Gray Buchanan," reported Vickers. "Discussions were inconclusive, and they broke down entirely when Father Buchanan locked the opposing negotiators in the church and tried to burn it down."

"Feelings still run high, then."

"Most decidedly, sir, yes."

41

"I realise that you weren't present for the match... you weren't present for the match, were you Vickers?"

"I was not."

"Of course. I realise that you weren't present for the match, but is there anything to these accusations of cheating?"

"It seems probable that the source of the dispute was a conflicting interpretation of the rules of the game," speculated Vickers.

"Ah, yes, of course," I realised. "I expect that officiating was in something of a state of flux in the day. Which rules even applied? St Andrews? Leith? Edinburgh?"

"Kidrummy and Kilcladdich."

"The villages shared their own rules?"

"Not precisely, sir, no," clarified Vickers. "The course crosses the river — the first nine holes were played by Kilcladdich rules, the remaining under those of Kildrummy."

"Devilish tenth fairway." From where I stood, the other side of the river was a good two hundred yards.

"Famously a par thirty-six," noted Vickers. "Until it was agreed, starting with the match in 1767, that the ninth hole and tenth tee ground should be on Moan Innes."

Vickers nodded toward the little island where, sure enough, the moss had been flattened into a rudimentary green, next to a mound of mud forming the tenth tee ground.

"Dare I ask..."

"It depends on the allegiances of the player," anticipated Vickers. "Anyone belonging to or invited to play by the MacAlistair family, for example, is subject to Kilcladdich rules when playing the ninth hole, otherwise Kildrummy rules apply."

"A very neat solution," I adjudged. "Every bit as stable and sane as the Alsace-Lorraine border. What happens when a neutral third party wants to play?"

"The Glen Glennegie golf course isn't tremendously popular outside of the immediate area."

"I won't say I'm surprised."

From where we stood on the river bank, there was a tiny pier, against which bumped a creaky, leaky dory. There were similar docks on Moan Innes and on the Kildrummy side of the river. From here, the banks rose towards the coastal road and bridge to form a deepish, steepish gorge where the river passed behind the Kilcladdich distillery.

As we walked up the grade, accompanied by the bells and baas of my followers, Vickers had an epiphany.

"The golf balls were on the floor of your room."

"How peculiar," I said. "Perhaps it's some sort of clue. They weren't spelling out a name, were they? Or laid out in a likeness of the deceased?"

"They were distributed most randomly," said Vickers, "giving very much the impression that they had been dropped accidentally."

"Sound reasoning, Vickers. Was the room not locked?"

"It was not," said Vickers, glancing with concern towards the Mash and Mashie which, as we'd now nearly arrived at the road, was out of sight behind the distillery. "That's why I came looking for you, so that I might retrieve the key."

"Yes, I follow your line of reasoning, Vickers, and see in it only one flaw. I don't have the key. You do."

"I'm loath to contradict you, sir..." Vickers produced two heavy church keys from his waistcoat. "...neither of these fit the door."

"I think I might be beginning to see the light, now Vickers," I said. "Tell me, did you make up the bed?"

"It was already made up, I believe."

"But you removed the bottle of whisky from the nightstand."

"There was no bottle on the nightstand."

"Right oh," I said. "What about the fort I made out of cushions and the wireless cabinet — you didn't dismantle it, did you?"

"There was no such structure..." Vickers raised his eyebrows in surprise surmise. "Oh dear."

"No harm done, Vickers. If you can recall what room you were in, you can simply return the golf balls, with our apologies."

"Indeed, sir. I believe that I should see to that immediately."

"No rush, Vickers. How urgent have golf balls ever been in anyone's life? I mean, anyone that shouldn't know better."

"It's not so much the return of the golf balls which concerns me, but the retrieval of your socks and undergarments."

"Oh, right. Yes, that could probably stand looking into sooner rather than later," I agreed. "One final point on this whole secret process, though, if you will, Vickers. The broad consensus now is that there is no such thing."

"Your father believed that there was."

"Eh? My father had a view on the question?"

"He did." Vickers fiddled distractedly with the golf balls in his pocket, doubtless dwelling on misfiled socks and smalls. "When we visited for the tasting in 1909 — you were too young to accompany your father, and instead were sent to Reims Conservatory for Champagne Recognition and Appreciation — Mister Boisjoly tasted pre-match whisky, as did Mister Tibbits and Mister Sheercliffe, and they all agreed that it was distinct — and distinctly superior — to subsequent years, in some fashion that must have been the result of some key element."

"Not to interrupt you, Vickers," I interrupted, "but are you saying that somewhere in this town there is or, before my father got to it, there was a 150-year-old bottle of Glen Glennegie?"

"Oh, yes, sir — an entire case remained, at the time, but when we returned ten years ago there was a mishap of some sort, and it was mislaid."

CHAPTER FIVE

The Long-Standing Grudge of Constable Budge

Sunrise, according to all available accounts, had occurred. I'm a trusting soul and so I believed that, in spite of a comprehensive absence of anything that might be called empirical evidence, such as a glimmer at the window of the Mash and Mashie to light me to breakfast.

Nevertheless, I found my way to smokies and scones and steaming pots of eye-opener, arrayed in simple abundance along the bar.

If there was anyone behind the bar I couldn't see him for the buffet, and either the other guests had already eaten or were still in bed. And so my energies and attention were focused exclusively on a deserving crisp of smoked haddock when the door opened, welcoming a whirl of wet wind and a dark silhouette. The shadow stepped into the firelit yellow of the bar room, and said a most unexpected thing.

"Oh, hives and pize — Anthony Boisjoly."

"What ho, Budgers." I think I recognised him by reflex — the last and only time I ever saw a policeman in Kilcladdich was this very same Constable Hamish Budge, called out to adjudicate the not-entirely-condoned construction of a toll booth on Glen Glennegie bridge and, tangentially, to repeat in open court the story of Molly MacAlistair and the vicar. Other than that, I might have been at a loss — he was the same solid, well-nourished constable he'd been ten years ago, but he was draped in an immense greatcoat, complete with riding cape, and he'd somehow trained a wild moustache — very much in the tradition of the English garden — to remain at rest on his upper lip. There was still about him, though, the rosy-cheeked boy policeman, perhaps even more so now, as he presented as if he'd found the cape and moustache in a trunk in his grandfather's attic.

45

"I might have known I'd find you here," complained Budge. "Ten years to the day. I haven't had cause to come out to Glen Glennegie in ten years and when I do, there's a Boisjoly."

"I know," I agreed. "I can hardly believe my luck either. How are you, Constable?"

"Detective Sergeant."

"How are you, Detective Sergeant? Tea? Smokie?"

"Mister Boisjoly, I'm here investigating a suspicious death."

"I know you are," I said, switching on a bit of solemnity. "Lummy MacAlistair. It was my idea that the authorities be called in."

"Did you do it?"

"I did not," I confessed, for now was a time for candour. "But I respect your initiative very much. You never know when you might catch out the guilty party with a surprise direct question. How do you take it? Sweet with milk, if memory serves."

"All right, go on then." Budge swung his elaborate outer cladding onto a nearby chair and took another for himself. "Where were you when it happened?"

"On a train, just north of Stirling. Can't say where, exactly, but I recall passing a river, if that helps, and a mill."

"And what are you doing here?"

"Same thing I was last time you saw me."

"Blocking a public thoroughfare and creating a common nuisance?"

"I mean, in addition to that," I clarified. "I've inherited my father's place on the Glen Glennegie jury."

"Oh, yes?" Budge burrowed into this overcoat and withdrew a notepad. "Does that mean that Sheercliffe sot is here too? And that Tibbits lunatic?"

"In fond memory and spirit," I said. "Otherwise, no. The Tibbits interests are represented ably by his daughter, Tiana 'Tannin' Tibbits, and Mister Sheercliffe's wife Shelby has taken his ample seat on the jury."

"Very good then." Budge wrote down these names with a professional enthusiasm, as though recording an eye-witness statement. "Londoners, I take it, like you."

"Like me?" I queried. "I think we both know that's as near impossible as makes no difference, but yes, they're from the big smoke."

"Londoners." Budge said the word with an intonation not dissimilar to the one employed by Londoners when they say the word 'lawyers'. "Coming up here and judging Scotch whisky."

"Yes, I agree that on the surface that sounds almost deliberately absurd, but I believe the distance is the point — competitors and their kin aren't famous for their cold-blooded neutrality."

Budge stirred his tea and expelled a cynical air formed by a complex orchestration of breath and cheek and lip, like an adolescent pony that's stopped believing.

"Where do I find these other two Londoners?"

"Three, if you count my man, Vickers," I replied. "We're all staying here."

"I take it Vickers was on the train with you this morning?"

"He was," I said. "Sound asleep, too. So was Tannin. On the train, I mean. She was wide awake and making cogent observations about the scenery."

"So that just leaves…" Budge glanced at his notes. "…Shelby Sheercliffe."

"Or any number of others who were on hand when it happened."

Budge didn't answer in words. He just drew meaningfully on his tea and fixed me with an eye that said 'Londoners' as clearly as if he'd spat the word on the floor.

"I take it you found the flare?" I presumed.

"I did," confirmed Budge. "Badly damaged by water, but it had clearly been fired just prior to that."

"Kilcladdich doesn't have a fire department, as such," I explained. "But it does have several water silos, usually well supplied with river water. Doubtless they saw the fire, they saw the water tower, and you know the old axiom; when all you have is an immense amount of water, every problem looks like a fire."

"It wasn't a fire, though, was it?"

"Wasn't it? There was rather a lot of smoke, and my understanding is that 'where there's smoke, there's fire' is one of the laws of Thermodynamics. Newton said it, I believe, with respect to some very fishy behaviour on the part of his next-door neighbour but one."

"There was fire, yes, but it was a byproduct of the explosion."

"Ah, I take your meaning."

"Fire would have burned out on its own," continued Budge. "But the damage was well done already."

"Yes, I imagine it was." I took a pointedly non-inquisitive sip of tea. "Any idea what caused it?"

"Methanol, exposed to the open air, and a powerful catalyst — the flare."

"And how do we think methanol was exposed to the air?" I asked. "The still is air-tight."

"Clearly, Mister Boisjoly, it was not." Budge leaned away in his chair and brought his tea with him. "There are signs that Mister MacAlistair was employing unconventional distilling methods."

"Oh, yes? Such as?"

"Such as physical evidence and clues that are entirely none of your business, Mister Boisjoly."

"Oh, do come along, Budgers. I told you the one about Molly MacAlistair and the vicar."

"No you didn't," countered Budge. "That was Lummy MacAlistair. Over a game of whist... and you weren't even there."

"I had a prior commitment with a set of bagpipes," I said, coolly. "In any case, I took full responsibility — in open court — for telling you the one about Molly MacAlistair and the vicar, and that was entirely due to your charming but occasionally ill-timed — such as, for a handy example, while in open court —

outspokenness. I'd have thought you'd have considered us whisper-sisters, after all that."

Budge looked about the empty room. "I suppose it won't do any harm. Obviously the killer already knows what happened."

"There you go."

"It looks as though Lummy MacAlistair was redistilling the methanol," confided Budge.

"Intriguing," I said. "Except, Budgit, isn't that common practice?"

"It is, yes," he agreed. "The head is often run through the still three or four times to capture any ethanol and traces of malt, but it appears that Lummy may have been air-filtering it, at the same time."

"To what end?"

"I can't say for certain," said Budge, with a speculative squint, "but a possibility strongly suggests itself in the form of a flue mechanism, by which Lummy controlled the air that flowed to the furnace."

"Again, this strikes me as not only forgivable but, indeed, indispensable," I opined. "Some means is required to control the temperature, in aid of progressively raising it to separate the head and heart."

"Yes, but the flue exhausts into the upper floor of the distillery." Budge emphasised this telling observation with a jab of his teacup in my general direction. "It would have filled the room with smoke."

"Morning Anty. Are those smokies?" The stairs, next to the bar and leading to the guest rooms, were very suddenly all bright and Tibbity.

"Morning Tanners," I echoed. "Smokies as crispy as burnt bark, circular bacon as round and sound as a pound, pudding as black as the heart of a Londoner. Tea?"

"Please."

"In the meantime, you probably won't remember Constable Budge, which is just as well, for he is no longer — Tannin Tibbits, meet Detective Sergeant Budge."

"I understand that you were on the train with Mister Boisjoly during the explosion yesterday, Miss." Budge started in with the officiousness right out of the gate.

"I think so." Tannin spoke distractedly as she inspected the buffet. "We only have the word of half the town when the explosion occurred, but it stands to reason."

"In that case, would you happen to know where I could find Mrs Shelby Sheercliffe?" asked Budge.

"On the links." Tannin spoke with the grace of a girl who knows how to articulate with a rasher or two of bacon in her mouth. "She knocked on my door at some insane hour — nine-thirty, I think — and asked if I wanted to join her."

"Very good." Budge stood and drained his teacup with the commanding majesty of a big game hunter, taking a last drop of Sunday tiffin gimlet from atop an elephant. "I'll ask you both to remain on hand for the duration of the investigation." He upholstered himself into his greatcoat, nearly doubling his wing span, and charged out into the elements.

"Was that the chap who pinched you and papa for some unspeakable debauchery in 1919?" asked Tannin from the outside of a handful of haddock. "I was too young to attend court, but everyone said it was better than a panto."

"It was, I expect, depending on one's perspective," I agreed. "From the view of the gallery, for example, a panto is always a treat. For the chap playing the back end of the horse, however, the experience can be inconsistent."

"What was your role?"

"I played the hero in the dock, pleading guilty to quaint regional misdemeanours, some of which I'd never heard, and many of which I'm convinced were invented for the occasion." I apportioned two fresh cups of tea. "However, the more immediate consequence of that whole, blurry, non-sequential series of events, is that it's left Detective Sergeant Budge with a pronounced prejudice against Londoners."

"Well, how unfair is that?"

"Exactly."

"Mind you, having said that…"

"No, I know, grain of truth in everything," I acknowledged. "But in this case it means that the investigation into the mysterious death of Lummy MacAlistair will be done with blinders on."

"He thinks one of us did it?" asked Tannin. "But we weren't even here."

"No, I know, but that still leaves Shelby."

"Doubtless she'll be able to account for her activities at the time." Tannin shrugged happily at a stick of smoked haddock held aloft — like many well-bred girls who find themselves abroad at breakfast, she ate with gusto, and with her fingers.

"That's just it," I countered. "She can't. According to the bickering barkeeps, they would have seen anyone who had been close enough to the distillery to shoot a flare through those little vents."

"Tough shot at any distance," estimated Tannin.

"Exactly. And the only blind spot is the other side of the distillery, between the building and the gorge."

"Does that prove something?" asked Tannin.

"On its own, no," I replied. "But when Budge asks her, Shelby's going to tell him that she was alone on the sixth tee ground, and that there was no one behind the distillery."

"But you just said that there must have been."

"No," I gently corrected, "I said that what we have here is a seemingly impossible locked-room mystery."

"Unless she did it."

"Unless, as you say, she did it," I conceded. "Which is exactly what Detective Sergeant Budge will conclude. He is clearly a man of many and varied gifts, so much so that he must discipline them all with an unyielding focus on presupposition. This is the way with many in his trade."

Tannin reflected on this and simultaneously formed an ingenious sandwich of tatties and herring.

"What is it you think he might overlook?"

"That, I cannot say." I stopped for a sage sip of sinensis. "It's rather in the nature of a mystery that, particularly in the early stages, one does not know what one does not know."

"Talking of which," chewed Tannin, thoughtfully, "that's one thing Budge hasn't considered, if he thinks Shelby did it."

"What's that?"

"Whoever did it knows the whisky-making process," said Tannin, adroitly adding a round of bacon to her sandwich mid-flight. "Shelby, expert as she may be at golf and not falling off mountains and doubtless a thousand other terribly useful things, doesn't know distillation from dishwater."

"You know something, young Tanners," I reflected, "you don't half remind me of a fuller-lipped, longer-lashed version of myself in my salad days. Have you ever done any detecting?"

"I used to be a dab hand at finding my father's hat and umbrella the next day."

"That's excellent training for the first division," I said. "Ever find his shoes on the roof?"

"No, but with surprising regularity in the coal chute."

"Very common. Comes from trying to sneak in quietly, after having left the house keys in the taxi."

"But of course." Tannin cleared her palate with a hearty swallow of tea. "You really do have a knack for this, Anty."

"As do you." A Boisjoly can give, after all, as good as he gets. "And normally, when approaching a problem of this nature, I do so as the wittier, more urbane partner in a sort of mystery-solving cross-talk act with an investigating detective."

"You're going to team up with Budgie?" asked Tannin.

"I'm not. I believe that he and I will be more productive pursuing different orbits, intersecting occasionally for a warm 'ahoy' and exchange of ideas, in the pattern of distant esteem set by Saturn and Jupiter." I poured two momentous cups of tea. "I propose to team up with you."

"Well, you could do worse." Tannin squinted thoughtfully over her tea. "That Ludio bloke, for instance. Has he always been like that?"

"Without knowing to what you refer, exactly, I'm going to say yes, he has. What did he do?"

"Nothing very, very odd," she allowed, in the tone of one being deliberately broad-minded. "He knocked on my door last night."

"He's harmless," I explained. "He's probably just fallen in love with you. Perfectly understandable. I toyed with the idea myself, briefly, when we were on the train."

"Oh, right." Tannin swirled her tea distractedly. "What saved you, in the end? Was it the way I ate all your salted almonds? I couldn't stop. I was like a girl possessed."

"Professional ethics," I explained. "When you told me that you were serving on the jury with me, I sacrificed my personal predilection for the greater good."

"Glen Glennegie." Tannin spoke this as a toast and raised her cup. "That's just it, though, you recall yesterday, when Molly MacAlistair found the lot of us in the distillery, and I pretended to be soft-centred for Ludovic?"

"I do."

"He thought I was serious, I think. He came round last night to let me down easy. His heart belongs to Isabette."

"What did he say, exactly?"

"Not sure, now, but it rhymed."

"He hasn't let on to Molly, though."

"No." Tannin squinted into the past. "No, in fact, he asked me to continue to wear the mask, if I could bear it, to keep Molly from twigging."

"That's all right then." I leaned into the table, creating a zone of confidentiality that encompassed Tannin and our teacups. "This will ingratiate you with the MacAlistair camp, just as the perception that a romance exists between Isabette and myself will smooth my way with the MacAngus partisans."

"I don't know that I want my romance with Ludio, fictional or otherwise, to be widely reported."

"No, I agree you have the heavier reputational burden to bear," I sympathised. "And indeed, while Isabette is a rippin'

53

pippin, with all the bits in just the right order and quantity, her mother has a way of looking at a chap as either loose or landed. We must tread a narrow path — not so truthful on our part that it suppresses it in others, but not so convincing, either, that I end up sentenced to life with Isabette without due process."

"Oh, right oh, then." Tannin leaned back in her chair, lapsing dangerously outside of the confidentiality zone. "So, what do we do, exactly? Just sort of, ask people if they killed Lummy MacAlistair?"

"If you think that'll work," I said. "You'll always want to be reading your audience. I will often distract and guide with relevant and revealing anecdotes."

"You like to tell stories."

"I do."

"I think I noticed that on the train coming up," recalled Tannin. "How many members does your gentlemen's club have, anyway?"

"We have a number of affiliates."

"Very well, Anty, I'm in." Tannin raised her cup in a toast. "You take the high road, and I'll take the low road..."

"...and we'll solve this murder 'afore Budge."

CHAPTER SIX

Barribault's Better Bitter

To obscure the collusion, and because Tannin still had some important work to do with a Lorne sausage, I left the pub first.

The road to Kildrummy was teeming with emptiness. I confess, I felt a trace of melancholy that my sheep had apparently elected, literally overnight, to operate under new management. The sentiment was short-lived and I was instead soon overcome by the awesome burden of office as I passed the urban side of the pub, characterised by a waving meadowland, where a herd of perhaps two dozen sheep lay in wait. The littlest of them, working a lucrative arbitrage in the overlooked grassy bits between his siblings, spotted me first and leapt happily onto the road. In a moment, the news of the outing spread throughout the community, and I was leading a clattering, clanging cloud towards Kildrummy.

Jolly as all this shepherding was, it wasn't entirely in keeping with the low-key tone that most experts agree is vital to a quality rural investigation. So, I slowed as I passed the door of the MacAlistair distillery and then stopped, turned, and gazed inquisitively back up the road. Following the dictates of tradition, the sheep did the same, and in that instant I dashed behind the distillery and onto the golf course, where I immediately upset Shelby Sheercliffe's approach, causing her to hook badly to the right of the third green. The ball struck a dead elm with a very satisfying 'toc', rebounded in a magnificent arc overhead, and landed about three yards behind us.

"I think that entitles me to a Mulligan," judged Shelby.

"You can make it a double," I said, munificently. "A Boisjoly knows how to set things right."

"I mean I'm allowed to retake the shot," clarified Shelby, and then appeared to quote, *"'At the player's pleasure might a stroke be tooken again, without penalty, from where lyeth the ball or where layeth the ball, should an honest strike be distrayed by beast, imbecile, or feeble-minded child.'"* Shelby studied my face, as though in aid of making a dispassionate categorisation. "Or is that Kildrummy rules?"

"Is there a material difference?"

"Oh, yes," Shelby assured me. "One side or the other — I can't remember which — before taking the shot, I'd be required to tie you to a post or a tree, or arrange to have you shut up in a barn."

"How could you possibly know that?" I asked.

"Pure chance. That one stayed with me because it's right before what you do when your ball is claimed by a hen, and right after your options in the case a match is suspended due to Jacobite uprising."

"No, I mean, how is it that you know the rules at all?"

"I've read them, of course." Shelby, having apparently decided to err on the side of convenience, putted her ball back to roughly where it had been when I arrived. "Both sets of rules are at the pub, available for public consultation during opening hours. That's one of the few common rules."

"I understand the temptation to set oneself apart." I stepped back as I spoke, giving Shelby scope in which to express herself in practice strokes. "But there's a danger in distinction. Take the case of Quattro's and the American Bar at the Wittlepool Hotel. Both bars claimed to have originated a concoction they called the Bitter Spill and, to be fair, they probably did, wherein lay the problem; two delicious and hard-working cocktails, independently devised, with the same name but — and this is the key factor of the story — completely different recipes."

"I don't know that it's the same thing." Shelby spoke to me, I believe, but addressed her ball.

"Not strictly apples to apples, no," I agreed. "But the core message is sound. Say a chap is in the habit of taking his afternoon refresher at Wittlepool's, but finds himself at Quattro's just before an important court appearance or pivotal darts match. He orders what he expects to be a bolstering combination of Angostura bitters, gin, seltzer, and lime cordial, and is delivered instead a quart of bitter and stout, carefully layered to create a clever sunset effect. There is, naturally, discord, arguments, demands for compensation, severe questions asked in the House of Lords. You can see where this is going."

"No, in point of fact, Mister Boisjoly, I can't."

"Vox populi," I elucidated. "What Adam Smith would call the invisible hand of the market, although there's little evidence the man ever set foot in either establishment. Quattro's and Wittlepool's each stood by their claim to the name, you see, so the drinking man decided which was to be the spiritual home of the Bitter Spill — neither. Quattro's version became known as Quitter's Swill, and Wittlepool's as the Spittlepool. Both drinks soon died out in popularity, after that, and to garnish the tale with a sweet irony, Barribault's revived the name last year as a virgin cocktail for children and the friendless."

Anyone observing from a distance would have assumed that Shelby hadn't been listening, because the epilogue coincided exactly with a cracking great thwack, and she let fly her ball in a positively inspirational trajectory from where she stood to not two yards from the hole.

"Well, the Glen Glennegie course rules have been divided now for some hundred and fifty years." Shelby dropped her quibbly or spickle-spoon or whatever it was into her golf bag with what a cynic might describe as studied nonchalance. "If the voice of the people was ever going to force a solution on Kildrummy and Kilcladdich, you'd think it would have happened by now."

"The lesson of the parable is compromise."

"No it isn't." Shelby hefted her golf bag onto her shoulder. "The lesson is opportunity, and the squandering thereof." She strutted toward the third green and I kept pace. "You know what they should have done? Quattro's or Wittlepool's? They should have made an offer to buy or sell the name, then both parties would have profited."

"I see your point."

"Take this course." Shelby stopped to helpfully point out the links with an expansive gesture. "Toughest eighteen holes I've ever played. If they just standardised on St Andrew's — or any set of rules, for that matter — there'd be queues from the pub to the first fairway. The bogie of Glen Glennegie would be the man to beat for all of Scotland."

As she walked, Shelby scanned the links, doubtless planning twelve moves ahead, like all good golfers and chess masters. Something caught her eye, and she stopped.

"I was there, at the sixth tee ground." She pointed in the direction indicated.

"During the explosion, you mean."

"Exactly." She turned 180 degrees and looked back at the distillery. "I'd have seen anyone between the distillery and the gorge. And I watched until the fire brigade showed, some ten minutes later. They'd have seen me — I told that bureaucrat to ask them."

"I take it you've been speaking with Detective Sergeant Budge."

Shelby nodded distractedly. "Asked the same questions, eight different ways, and no matter what I said he'd reply, 'oh-ho', and write something in his blasted notebook."

"Oh-ho, you say," I repeated. "Not, ah-ha, or mm-hmmm?"

"Oh-ho. Quite sure. Why?"

"Mister Budge is a man of hidden depths."

"You know him?"

"We go way back. We were in the panto together."

"Oh, right." Shelby nodded knowingly. "I think he mentioned that. Molly and the vicar."

"That was Lummy."

"I heard that you swore under oath that it was you."

"Yes, that's true, but only in the technical and legal sense."

"What other sense is there?"

"Moral," I said, with the cool indifference of a just man wrongly accused.

"I agree." Shelby issued one of those crooked, meaningful smiles that make blackmailers so famously well-loved. "It's very useful to know who can be trusted with a secret."

Shelby paced off towards the third green, expressing with her gait designs on the ball that I don't believe it deserved.

I retreated the other way, towards what would be the back of the distillery, if where Angus and Alistair had been, and where the sheep were now, was the front. From there I maintained the blind spot and walked toward the gorge. There was no escaping the fact that Shelby would have seen anyone assuming, of course, that she was looking. I couldn't see the sheep from where I stood next to the valley's edge, and so they couldn't see me, and so neither would have Angus nor Alistair. On the other hand, there was nowhere to go — the gorge wasn't so deep as a quarry, say, nor sheer as a sheet of glass, but neither was it a rolling meadow of pillowy shrubbery.

As I moved my way up the hill towards the road I noted that the sheep had gone. Melancholy work, outwitting the poor creatures like that, but it had to be done. I climbed up to the road and set out across the bridge, where the herd, now numbering at least forty sheep, cheerfully waited for me. I led them to Kildrummy.

The MacAngus distillery was much like the MacAlistair distillery — two stories low and wide as a barn, wearing a conical chimney on its sloping top. It was across the road from the MacAngus malt house and distinguishable as the one that was puffing out fluffy white clouds of peaty, aromatic smoke. I would knock on the door at some point in the near term, but foggy recollections of Kildrummy diplomatic relations told me to get my visa stamped by the family matriarch first.

The last time I visited Yvaine at home, I was underneath her window, stood on a hay wagon, and torturing a bagpipe. I felt a frank exchange of ideas with the woman was very much dependent on presenting as a saner, more sober and less impetuous Anty Boisjoly. In aid of projecting and protecting this image, therefore, I had forty-odd more sheep than required.

I jogged on, pursued by clanging bells and clattering hooves and a plaintive baaing that seemed to chorus 'Anty, wait, no, we're back here... Anty... please don't abaaaaandon us...'

Finally, I spotted an appetising meadow behind a high stone and harling cottage, and was inspired to a new tack. I allowed the flock to close the distance a bit, and then led them across the curtilage and onto the meadow, which turned out to be more of a garden. I continued behind the house and waited for the congregation to arrive.

"Right, well, you must be hungry after all that running about," I said, but the sheep weren't ready to settle in. They were still panting for the chase, on edge, pricked of ear and waggly of tail, and clearly in no trusting mood.

"But look at all this delightful nosh." I gestured at the varied and plentiful greenery. The sheep followed my movements but remained unimpressed. I tore a leaf from a nearby plant and demonstrated the technique.

"Mmm," I lied. "Delicious. Not entirely ripe, I won't deceive you, but not without a certain honest country gusto."

"Mister Boisjoly?"

This rather took me by surprise. About me were only sheep, and they seemed as confused by the address as I was.

"What are you doing in my garden?" asked the disembodied voice. "Again." And I knew in an instant that I was once more beneath the window of Yvaine MacAngus.

"Oh, what ho, Mrs. MacAngus." I looked up at her, leaning out of her window with a decidedly judgemental air.

"Where did all those sheep come from?"

"Sheep?" I dodged, I think, expertly.

"All those sheep, eating the heads off my sweet potatoes."

"Oh, right. Sheep. Are they not yours?"

She didn't answer. Instead Yvaine just rested what I would call a fatigued gaze upon me.

"Have you come looking for Isabette?" she asked at length, doubtless after a titanic battle of will, recalling her intention to help push along my romance with her daughter. "She's not here, I'm afraid, but I'll put the kettle on if you'd like to wait."

"That would be most welcome."

"There was never a hundred-and-fifty-year-old case of Kilcladdich." Yvaine made this clear contention from the other side of a multi-tiered tea caddy, with shelves stocked with scones and shortbreads. The MacAngus salon, which I was seeing for the first time, was a similarly elaborate but ordered gallery of golf memorabilia — trophies and clubs and group photographs of pivotal ladies' tournaments. Yvaine herself had braided her angry red hair into what looked an effective horse whip, and she was wearing a skirt of what I assume was MacAngus tartan. Her talent for presentation was prodigious, and inversely proportional to her gifts for baking, but I found that if discreetly but thoroughly soaked in tea and gripped firmly, her shortbread biscuits could be broken down to bite-sized rubble.

"I thought as much," I lamented. "Too good to be true."

"Oh, no, the case exists," confounded Yvaine, but then went on to explain, "Or at any rate, it did, but it wasn't Kilcladdich nor Kildrummy. Back then it was all Glen Glennegie."

"So this rivalry hasn't been with us since the dawn of time," I concluded.

"No, that nonsense started in 1839," deplored Yvaine, "with that dire golf match."

"The famous match that divided preferential choice of the waters and the peat." I surmised.

"Aye. That match."

"My staff antiquarian tells me that the date of the match was 1767."

"And so it was." Yvaine's resentment for the whole, grim affair was expressed in the snapping of a shortbread, which sent a crumb whistling past my ear and across the room, where it embedded itself in the wall. "Kilcladdich started labelling their whisky 'Original Glen Glennegie', and Kildrummy called its own 'Authentic Glen Glennegie'."

"I see how that might get out of hand."

"And get out of hand it did. Soon enough, bottles of Kilcladdich were turning up in London labelled 'Non-toxic Glen Glennegie' and Kildrummy, obviously, responded with 'Glen Glennegie Reserve — for Scots only'. Very effective campaign, that was."

"I don't doubt it," I said. "So, you had another war of attrition on your hands, doing neither side any good."

"Exactly so. Finally, the distributors made it clear they'd stop buying from either distillery unless they sorted themselves out, but they simply could not forget that golf match, so rather than just go back to everyone making as much Glen Glennegie as they could sell, the master distillers challenged each other to this competition, once every decade."

"Whatever made them agree to such a thing?"

"Pride." Gesturing to emphasise the point, Yvaine allowed a piece of shortbread to fall onto her saucer, which broke in two. "Master distillers pass the skills, the position, and the bone-headed conceit down the generations. Naturally, neither side was prepared to admit he'd lose such a competition, so both sides readily agreed to it."

"I confess, it's worked well for me," I said. "Gets me out of the house every now and then, and the Glen Glennegie jury of three members is the most exclusive club to which I belong, right after the London Chapter of the Society of Chaps Who Don't See the Point in Complaining About the Weather."

"When it started out there were dozens of you." Yvaine nodded a cynical, resigned sort of nod. The kind of nod that says not so much 'yes' as 'pssh'. "One representative from each distributor. Now there's just the one, and you and that Sheercliffe woman."

"Couldn't handle the strict training schedule?" I guessed. "I remember Papa used to work tirelessly, sometimes late into the night, on his whisky appreciation skills."

"They lost interest," corrected Yvaine. "There was less and less whisky to distribute, so there were fewer and fewer distributors."

"I don't see how that follows. The grain still grows, the water flows, the barrels repose... what changed?"

"Everything." Yvaine absently tried to bite a scone, failed, and then just looked at it with a sweet melancholy. "To start, they say the whisky was never the same since that game. Whether or not that's true, productivity dropped off, costs went up — it's what happens when a once-great distillery splits in two and goes into competition with itself."

"I'm particularly intrigued by this idea that something fundamental changed in the whisky," I said, idly stirring my tea with a thin brick of shortbread. "Especially with regards to this secret process."

"There was never any secret process," insisted Yvaine. "Though, now you mention it, I wouldn't wonder if Duncan was starting to believe there was."

"Oh, yes? What has he said to make you think that?"

"Not a thing," mused Yvaine. "Doesn't say anything about anything, in fact, but he just seems more secretive than ever."

"How so?"

"Well, last night, he opened the door a crack when I brought him some baking." To demonstrate the notion, Yvaine, with some effort, raised a plate of scones. "But this morning he wanted his axe, for some reason, and a hammer and chisel, and he made me leave them outside."

"You don't say."

"The point is, up until now he's only been acting like he had a secret." Yvaine looked cautiously about the room and cocked her head to listen to the sheep calling out for me. "Now, if you see the distinction, he's acting like he actually has a secret."

CHAPTER SEVEN

The Case of the Case of the Case of Kildrummy

I left Yvaine's house by the side door, where the sheep had posted an honour guard — a dizzy, dopey, crudely-sheared billow with a lazy eye and protruding tongue. He dutifully called out for the others and we reconvened on the parade route.

"At ease," I called as we arrived once again at the MacAngus distillery. "I must pay a personal call. Feel free to speak amongst yourselves."

I tapped up the steps to the distillery floor and rapped a discreetly coded 'what ho' on the door.

"Go away." This was, I reasoned, Duncan. There was a flat, matter-of-factness about his tone, rather as though he meant to say 'just a moment' and instead had accidentally said 'push off.' I took encouragement from that.

"'Morning, Mister MacAngus. It's Anthony Boisjoly. Let's make it Anty, shall we, for I know you're a busy man."

There was a bit of movement — shuffling and footsteps and the like approaching the door — and then a hushed, measured voice, "Forgive me, I was on the other side of the still."

"Not at all," I replied.

"Doubtless I was unclear," continued Duncan. "What I meant to convey was that you should go away. Now, go away."

"I wonder if you might spare me just a moment," I persisted. "Did you know that Lummy MacAlistair is dead?"

"I know that everyone's saying that Lummy MacAlistair is dead, and it might well be so," said Duncan with chatty calm. "I'm sure you'll understand; I'm not saying that you're a black-hearted spinner that would sooner tell ten tall tales than a single word of truth, only that you might well be."

"I'm afraid it's so, Mister MacAlistair. His distillery blew up."

"Aye, so I'm told." It was somehow clear from his voice that Duncan was nodding in an exaggerated fashion. "I'm also led to understand that two members of the Glen Glennegie jury are women, and that my niece, Isabette, is sweet on some lace-lined London pan-loafy."

"Ah…"

"And yet," continued Duncan. "I'm still not opening this door. So, do you think you can do better than any of that?"

"Well, in point of fact, I was hoping to discuss…" I lowered my voice at this point, I think, to imply an earnest respect for Duncan's fondly-held delusions. "…the process."

"What process?"

"I mean to say, the *process,*" I said, clearing up any confusion.

"Go away."

"I think there's a chance I know what it is," I persisted. "Or at any rate, what Lummy thought it was."

"So, what you're saying is that you can help me, by simply revealing some sort of secret process, make a whisky as good as that of Lummy MacAlistair's."

"Ehm…"

"Are you still there?"

"Just leaving, Mister MacAngus," I said. "One last thing — you know the candidate case of Kildrummy must be locked into the cabinet at the Mash and Mashie by four o'clock today, don't you?"

"Aye," replied Duncan. "And it'll be seen to, so long as I don't have too many more pointless conversations as the long day wears on." There was a short pause, measured in sarcasm. "Present company excluded, of course, Mister Boisjoly — this has been a most delightful and informative discussion."

"Oh, right…"

"Now, go away."

ꙮ

"Ya skillet-skulled spot of stubborn rust — a fellow'd be better asking a weather vane directions to the nearest mountain hare." Angus expressed this editorial view to Alistair from behind the bar at the Mash and Mashie, where I'd stopped for a pot of inspiration and a spot of information.

"Is that so, ya wax tea fork?" parried Alistair. "You haven't answered right since you last pointed left." Alistair returned his attention to me while Angus filled the pot. "Now, could you describe these sheep, Mister Boisjoly?"

"Well, yes, I suppose I could," I acknowledged. "But probably no better than could anyone who's never seen them. They're just sort of a lot of sheep, don't you know — woolly and white and displaying a marked absence of independent thinking."

"Could be Jock Mackie's lot…" reflected Alistair.

"More likely from the Findlay farm," opined Angus. "Were any of them wearing hats?"

"Hats?" I repeated, very much playing for time. "No, no hats. Is that very likely?"

"Not at all," said Angus. "But it would rule out any that we hadn't heard of."

"Yes, I daresay it would. They're just outside, if you'd like to have a look."

"You go, Angus," encouraged Alistair. "It'll give me a chance to put right the stocking you did this morning."

"I daren't leave you alone, Alistair, you know that," replied Angus in kind, "or you're likely to cut yourself on the spoons."

"Right oh." I took up my tray of tea. "Should anyone come in looking for a herd of sheep, you might direct him to me. There's an excellent chance that I can put him onto a good thing."

I joined Tannin at a table next to a fireplace crackling with coal.

"What ho, partner in crime-solving."

"What ho, Anty." She watched me lower the tray of tea to the table. "Oh, good. More tea."

"I know," I sympathised. "But we need clear heads, and it's not even four."

With this observation we both reflexively looked at the whisky cabinet, which still housed only the ten bottles of Kilcladdich.

"I spoke to Duncan," I said. "He claims that by some magic his candidate bottles will be presented in time."

"I thought he was locked into his distillery."

"He is," I confirmed. "Our interview was conducted through the door. I think this was for the best — he sounded unshaven."

"What did he have to say?"

"Little of substance," I recollected. "Indeed, it was in the main a series of counterpoints — he didn't believe that Lummy was dead, that you and Shelby were on the jury, that Isabette was romantically involved with a Boisjoly, and that there's any secret distillation process."

"Well, that's odd."

"Not so strange as all that. The families of many young ladies with whom I've been involved have expressed a similar unwillingness to believe their good fortune." I spoke distractedly, for I was pouring hot tea. "Sugar?"

"Please. I was referring to the secret process."

"Ah, yes, that bit is a little peculiar," I agreed. "Not least because Yvaine thinks that Duncan's starting to warm to the theory."

Our attention was drawn to a subdued but meaningful murmur as the door opened, amplifying the impatient grumbling from my followers. Molly came in and closed the door against them. She was draped in purple curtains and holding a hamper of pies at shoulder height.

"You know there's about a hundred sheep out there?"

"Free to a good home," I offered. "Provided they're not split up."

Molly gave me one of those indulgent smiles that I see so often, and asked the bar team for a neat Kilcladdich, causing Alistair to ring the bell which, going by the sheepish murmurs heard through the door, the flock interpreted as a great foretelling.

"You spoke to Yvaine, then." Tannin switched to barrister's waiting room voice.

"I did," I replied, in a similar volume. "I brought you back some shortbreads, by the way, in case you want to scratch your name into a bridge abutment."

"And I've been talking to Molly." Tannin peered down at her reflection in the teacup, but took the commitment no further. "You're right, she thinks of me as family, practically, and she was quite forthcoming. I think she's in the clear, by the way — she doesn't benefit from her husband's death."

"Who does?"

"Well, nobody, really. The distillery belongs to the whole family. In fact, without its master distiller, Kilcladdich can only suffer."

"Has Ludio not picked up the skills?"

A cloud passed over Tannin's face. "There was optimistic and, frankly, awkward talk of the hope invested in a future generation."

"That's interesting." I raised my tea and swirled it keenly. "Perhaps, then, Isabette and Ludio are exaggerating their need for secrecy."

"Oh, no." Tannin pointed at me with her spoon, which until then she'd been using to create amusing ripple effects in her teacup. "Molly was saying how glad she was that Ludio had found love outside of the village, given the limited opportunities for a lad of his — her words, not mine — elusive worth. She knows that Isabette is the only qualified candidate, and mentioned, apropos of that, how it happened once before."

"What happened once before?"

"Cross-Glennegie romance," explained Tannin. "This was thirty years ago — Lummy fell in love with a MacAngus."

"Lummy? Really?"

"So Molly tells it." Tannin smiled and waved vaguely at Molly across the bar room. "She's a pragmatic sort of widow, isn't she? It seems Lummy MacAlistair was once engaged to a girl named Fiona MacAngus."

"And the families managed to break it up?"

"They bought Lummy off. Sent the girl to Swiss boarding school. In irons."

"Lummy took money to end his relationship with Fiona?"

Tannin nodded. "Molly says they had an 'untroubled' marriage, but that Lummy had all the romance of kelp. Might not have been money, though — this was around the same time he became master distiller."

"So, perhaps something more valuable than money."

Tannin shrugged and curled her lip up at her tea, as though just that very instant realising that it was the runoff from boiled leaves.

"You enjoying your tea, Anty?" she asked.

"Haven't really given it much of a chance yet, if I'm honest."

"You know what it needs, I think?"

"Milk?"

"Milk, sure, that might help." Tannin examined her tea from an angle. "Or Kildrummy '22 — a light, six year, woodsy, tea-time whisky."

I presented myself bar-side and ordered two Kildrummy '22 and water. Angus rang the bell and once again the sheep bustled and baad outside in a manner suggestive of a restive audience of theatre-goers, impatient in the foyer on opening night.

"So, are we ruling out Molly and Ludio?" Tannin added a precise one-to-two of water to her whisky.

"As a rule, we don't rule anyone out until someone's been definitively ruled in," I said, mirroring Tannin's laboratory methodology. "However at the moment I'm pressed to imagine why either of them might have done it."

"Or how."

"Or how," I agreed. "But this problem applies to everyone."

"Except Shelby."

"Who also has no cause to kill anyone."

"Okay, so, what about the Kildrummy camp?" Tannin posed the question and then retreated into the atmosphere above her glass.

"Well, there's the obvious motive of competition," I said. "But I find that weak — the time to kill the Kilcladdich master distiller, if one were so inclined, was twenty years ago."

"It does seem notable that it happened right after he delivered his candidate bottles to the jury," observed Tannin. "What if Lummy really had discovered the secret process, and Duncan killed him for it?"

"Killing a chap, in my eerily broad experience of the field, is among the worst ways to get him to tell you a secret."

"Oh, right," conceded Tannin. "Well, what if they both discovered it and Duncan wanted to keep it for himself?"

"Better." I paused then, as did Tannin, for a sip of teatime whisky. "But again, the timing is too conspicuous to be ignored — after a hundred and fifty years, two people independently stumble on the same thing at the same time? The chances of that must be about one in heaps."

"Even then, how did he do it?" posited Tannin. "He was locked in his distillery."

"Well, of course, we have only his word for that," I said. "Although Yvaine says that she was having a shouty chat with him at the instant of the explosion."

"Does Duncan confirm the time?"

"I didn't ask him," I confessed. "But it stands to reason that Yvaine wouldn't have made the claim if she couldn't count on Duncan verifying it."

"Is that everyone then?"

"Isabette," I reminded her. "A dark horse outsider if ever there was one. I don't know if she's the type to kill, but I can attest first-hand that she's the type to throw a chap's shoes into the sea over a trifling misunderstanding."

"I suppose there's Angus and Alistair," noted Tannin.

"I suppose," I allowed. "Although I'm having difficulty bringing into sharp focus an image of them conspiring together on anything more coordinated than spillage."

The door opened again and Budge's greatcoat made an appearance. The detective sergeant himself was turned to the outside, speaking in pleading tones, "It's no use looking at me with those big wet eyes, you can't come in... You know, if it was up to me... I'm only enforcing the law..."

Budge entered, closed the door, pushed back up against it, and appeared to contemplate the inhumanity of it all.

"Whose sheep are those?"

"Are there sheep outside?" I asked. "Can you describe them?"

Budge assumed a smuggy bearing and swaggered over to our table.

"Morning Mister Boisjoly, Miss Tibbits." He liberated a chair from an adjacent table and made of himself a third. "Anything left in the pot?"

"I think so." I poured him a steaming portion. "Op, just enough. Maybe another four cups, at the very outside."

"Are you aware of your role in this investigation, Mister Boisjoly?" asked Budge as he removed his immense pelt.

"I think so," I said. "I'm the loveable scamp. You're the taciturn police sergeant with a secret but abiding respect and affection for me, and this is Miss Tibbits, my foil."

"Your role..." Budge spilt a slovenly spoon of sweet into his tea. "...no more and no less..." He cast in a careless clot of cream. "...is that of bystander."

"You see me more as a trenchant observer, you mean."

"No, I mean that you're to stop questioning witnesses, the both of you."

"Questioning witnesses?" I disdained. "Is that what you call taking tea with old acquaintances? Do you caution your mother of her right to counsel when you visit her at Christmas?"

"I understand, Mister Boisjoly..." Budge stirred his tea ominously, very much the way a man about to yell 'ah-ha!' would stir his tea. "...that you have resumed your practice of trifling with the affections of young ladies."

"Who said I ever stopped?"

"I thought as much. Heaven may marvel, what does a bonnie, bright girl like that want with a London extraneous like yourself."

"Isabette?" I asked. "If anything, Budgers, it's she who trifled with my affections. Gave me back my letters, but not without first reading them out loud in church." I took a strong restorative from my whisky before continuing. "This includes, I'll have you know, original poetry."

"I was led to understand that you and Isabette had rekindled your romance." There was a telling trace of optimism in Budge's otherwise studied indifference that recalled something to my mind — ten years previously, Budge had lingered for rather a while, considering his initial mandate was the merest dismantling of a toll booth formed of empty whisky crates. He even took a room at the Mash and Mashie and was, perhaps not matey as such, but not above fraternising with the locals and even the Londoners.

Something changed and I only in that moment realised that it was when Budge met Isabette and, simultaneously, discovered that she and I had sought and received her mother's permission to sit together at church. Constable Hyde took over in that instant, and I was pinched for what Budge later described in court as a 'profligate crime spree'. In a stroke, I had dashed his dreams and invested him with a lifelong antipathy towards Londoners.

"Oh, I say, Budgers, it's not like that at all. Isabette and I aren't..."

"More tea, DS?" popped off Tannin, raising the pot. "Oh, sorry Anty, I interrupted you. I believe that you were about to betray a confidence. Do carry on."

"I mean to say, Isabette and I, we're taking it slowly, don't you know. Older and wiser, and all that."

"Nothing I can do about that." Budge spoke with the tone of one who deplored the inadequacies of British law as it applied to Boisjolys and their kind. "But I will insist that you cease interfering in an active investigation."

"It's not interference, Budgie," said Tannin. "It's more... background research. Back label stuff."

"A bit of perspective," I added. "For instance, did you know that production at both distilleries has been deteriorating for decades?"

"And?"

"You don't find that interesting?"

"Should I?"

"Doesn't it suggest to you a possible motive for the murder of Lummy MacAlistair?" I asked.

"Perhaps..."

"This eternal and infernal competition has harmed both distilleries," I continued. "Profits are squeezed, customers are scarce, and the only thing that can save Glen Glennegie is an end to the feud."

"And how does the death of Lummy MacAlistair aid in that?"

"In two important ways." I cast a furtive eye at Molly, who was delivering meat pies to Angus from her hamper. "First, it's the master distillers — Lummy and Duncan, in the current generation — who are keeping this contest going. They could agree at any time to cooperate in the production of twice as much Glen Glennegie as one distillery can make on its own."

"And the other way?"

"As of latest dispatch, the MacAlistair distillery has no one to take over for Lummy," I said. "His death leaves the family in a weak negotiating position, should a merger be proposed."

"And you think Shelby Sheercliffe is going to propose such a merger?" Budge said this while nevertheless nodding just like a sane person.

"No, I'm not saying that — how does Mrs Sheercliffe enter into it?"

"She's the only one that could have done it, but I'll need a motive before arresting her," allowed Budge, munificently. "This just might do."

"I don't know." Tannin held up her glass and looked into it as one who sees a dark future in whisky. "I think that ship has sailed, Anty. As supplies dried up, so did the market — just because you make more Glen Glennegie doesn't mean you're going to sell it."

"There's always a market for quality whisky," I pronounced. "The Juniper club alone should be able to soak up anything not acquired by number fourteen, Gloucester Gardens."

"You and your club are valued customers, Anty, but even when Papa was here ten years ago he was struggling to find new markets," reported Tannin. "He had a very solid lead in the U.S., but, well, you know what happened there."

"What happened there?" asked Budge, apparently, sincerely.

"Prohibition," I said. "Surely you knew that America had gone dry."

"What do you mean, 'gone dry'. They've run out?"

"They've made alcohol illegal," clarified, she thought, Tannin.

"Still not quite getting you." Budge squinted at her. "How can you make alcohol illegal? How would you even enforce such a mad law?"

"He makes a good point," I noted. "I was in New York in '24 and, if anything, hooch was easier to come by than it is in London. And jolly good fun, too. I used to go to a speak called the Pious Protestant in the basement of a meatpackers on Gansevoort. They maintained a very strict password policy at the door. Every day they'd change the secret, you see, to some variation 'silk stockings' or 'American Telegraph at a dollar twelve', that sort of thing, and a network of well-placed informants would ensure that the police, and only the police, knew it. They always instantly knew who to turn away."

"How was the whisky?" asked Tannin.

"Unpredictable," I replied. "But they shared a house orchestra with the Waldorf, and they had a monkey that could pull pints."

"Just a minute now." Budge raised an official police pause hand. "You're saying that America has outlawed alcohol."

"That's right," confirmed Tannin.

"Not whisky."

"Especially whisky."

Budge sat back in his chair and stared straight ahead, processing this shift in his understanding of our cousins.

"There are speakeasies, as Anty says," continued Tannin. "And you can get whisky on prescription — doctors are making millions — and grocery stores sell powdered grape juice complete with a warning and the step-by-step instructions you need to avoid to prevent it turning into wine."

"Then, surely, they'll see what folly all this is," hoped Budge.

"They changed their constitution and everything."

"They'll just change it back."

"I don't think so, Budgie," differed Tannin. "They seem pretty happy with their bootleggers and bathtub champagne."

"Speaking as an officer of the law..." Budge broke his reverie. "...it can't last."

"Speaking as a distributor of whisky..." Tannin smiled a flat, resigned smile. "...I wish that were so."

Another rumble of sheepish discontent came to us as Yvaine, her hair swirling about her like a faithful fog formed of tomato soup, stepped quickly into the bar and closed the door very meaningfully in the face of several of my followers. Her cynical eye fell immediately on me.

"How many of those things have you got now?"

"I don't know," I said. "I tried counting them, but I fell asleep."

What happened next was a whip-quick series of events that unfolded so rapidly and chaotically that it's difficult now, recounting it all, to decide how to characterise it — mad, explosive, chaotic, or simply delightful? Certainly, it was a clockwork sequence, any slight departure from which would have resulted in completely different and far less entertaining results.

First, Yvaine crossed the bar and ordered a Kildrummy '26. Angus reached up for the bell key and, in that same instant, the door opened and Shelby swung in, robust and rollicking and carrying her golf bag, and in no great rush to close the door. Angus then rang the bell, and the sheep received that as a rallying cry. In an unbroken stream they thronged into the bar. In an instant there were sheep everywhere and they were happy, it seemed, merely to be invited. They didn't seek me out, particularly, and in fact flowed like liquid to all corners of the pub.

Angus, for some reason doubtless close to his heart, thought that the best reaction to this would be to continue ringing the bell, only louder. Possibly he thought it might frighten the sheep away or send up the alarm. If his intention was to attract more sheep, he must have been very satisfied with his efforts.

The bells and baaing and bustling of the bedlam reached a peak, boat race night measure of anarchy when Shelby closed the door, which was immediately opened again when Isabette, followed by more sheep, came into the pub. When they finally got the door closed again, Ludio came in.

Calm returned, some time later, when I, very much in the tradition of Hector's sacrifice for Troy, waded through the woolly waves and led my flock to the street. When I finally returned, there was a decidedly post-cataclysm, wide-eyed, disbelieving awe about the survivors. Bits of white fluff floated on the still air. Molly was standing on a table. Yvaine was sitting on the bar. Angus held the bell key tightly, but now in silent reflection. Shelby was practising short putts with an upturned whisky glass.

I expect it was the sudden return to normalcy that brought us all to gaze simultaneously on the one remaining anomaly in the room — in the candidate cabinet, still closed and locked, on the Kildrummy shelf, were ten duly tagged bottles. The clock on the wall showed two minutes to four.

CHAPTER EIGHT

The Peculiar Stipulations of the Golf Course Regulations

"Ya yard and a half of unravelled knitting," posited Alistair. "You've all the twig and grasp of a greased caber."

"Have I now, you imperial ounce of spent lees," queried Angus. "Then why don't you tell us what you saw?"

"I saw you ringing that bell like the neck of the chicken that beat you at draughts four games out of five."

This lively commerce in ideas had its wellspring in my curiosity about the mysterious appearance of ten bottles of Kildrummy. A pubbish serenity had been restored. Alistair was sweeping bits of wool from the floor. Angus was putting the furniture upright. I, having been asked explicitly to do as little as I could manage to do, was furthering my acquaintance with six-year Kildrummy '22. Everyone else had carried on with their days, in the main uninterested in how ten bottles of whisky had been placed in a locked cabinet while Angus held the key in his hand. Yvaine, certainly, was just happy that it was there, but she claimed no knowledge of how it came to be. No one else expressed tremendous interest in the remarkable illusion at all, much less a willingness to claim responsibility for it.

"And we're quite sure that's the only key." I defused, as I examined the bottles of Kildrummy. There were no obvious tricks to the cabinet. It was formed of thick glass walls on four sides, and it was fixed such that the bottom shelf was the surface of the bar, and it rose all the way to the ceiling.

"Aye," harmonised Angus and Alistair, with Angus providing the refrain, "It's never been off this hook, except for the tasting, and the nearest locksmith is in Baldibble."

"And the nearest locksmith that can copy that key died in 1902," added Alistair.

"Doesn't the mystery of the appearance of these bottles throw their authenticity into question?"

"Should it?" asked Angus, as he rehung a painting of Kilcladdich, as seen from Kildrummy in an earlier, happier day, with a shock of bluebells blowing on Moan Innes, and a flock of sheep that managed to graze without the guidance of a strong central government.

"I mean to say, you can't always trust an unlabelled bottle, can you?" I specified. "Only a few days before coming up I had some acquaintances round for a light lunch — just a little *confit de canard, petites pommes parisiennes,* small bun fight, that sort of thing. Vickers had decanted the *Chateau Sireine-sur-Sirein '15* and I had it all poured out before recognising it as *Cote Vaucharme '18.*"

"You don't say," said Alistair, flatly.

"I know — don't mention it to Vickers, by the way, we just soldiered on," I said in confidential tones. "And the gravy was brass polish, as it turns out, so hardly anyone noticed, in the end."

"That's Duncan's handwriting on the tag," declared Angus.

"And whatever's in those bottles," proclaimed Alistair, "that's the Kildrummy entry. Those are the rules."

"You can ask any magistrate, from Bow Street to Clerkenwell, there's no one with more respect for the rules than Anty Boisjoly," I contended. "Nevertheless, aren't these particular regulations getting a little crusty at the edges? Might be time for a review, what?"

"I don't think so," said Angus, while Alistair said, simultaneously, "I think not."

"No?" I asked. "You'd be surprised the difference a modest adjustment can make. In January, during the annual audit of the dress code at the Juniper — that's my club, you understand — we dropped a decades-long moratorium on school ties. Completely changed the atmosphere of the place — you'd think you were in Paris. And two of our oldest members discovered that they'd been best friends for five years at St Dunstan's."

"It's up to Duncan, at any rate." Alistair spoke with the aloof detachment of a man balancing a jumper-weight of wool on a dustpan.

"And Lummy." Angus spoke reflexively as he knocked the dust out of a seat cushion, but then he caught himself. "That is, I mean to say, the Kilcladdich master distiller."

"I understood that Lummy lacked an understudy," I said.

"True," mused Angus. "But there remain ten years before the jury sits again — that should be nearly enough time to train someone up."

"Aye," agreed Alistair. "It's Kilcladdich, after all. If no one turns up they can always get a blind tramp to randomly turn the valves. And, should no blind tramp be willing, Angus here could do it, under careful supervision."

"Speaking of rules," I spoke of rules, "I understand that both books of Glen Glennegie golf course regulations can be consulted here at the Mash and Mashie."

"Are you a golfer, Mister Boisjoly?" asked Alistair.

"Devotedly not."

"Then why would you want to see the rules, if you don't play?" asked Angus.

"Is that a requirement?" I asked. "At school, I was allowed — practically obliged, in fact — to read Machiavelli, and I've never established an authoritarian state. It's probably fair to say that the odds are less than even that I ever will."

"I suppose there's no wrong in it," adjudged Angus.

"That's just what Machiavelli said."

Alistair carried a ball of raw wool behind the bar and pushed it into a dustbin. Then he turned to a handsome oak cabinet and opened the doors to reveal a shelf of perhaps a dozen leather-bound notebooks beneath a snowy layer of dust.

"Blimey," I opined. "I had no idea. I'd pictured a couple of slim volumes. The entire Juniper darts rule book is only two dozen pages, and that's with the section setting out precisely what constitutes a legitimate target. An addendum made necessary, I confess, largely owing to my actions."

"Those are tournament reports, and editions of the rules dating back to 1740." Alistair withdrew two modest volumes. "You'll want the latest, I take it."

"I will," I agreed. "So, the course rules are, in fact, subject to change."

"Of course."

"Then why don't they simply change them to be the same?"

"You'd have to ask the tee ladies," interjected Angus.

"The tea ladies set the course rules? Golf culture really is an undiscovered continent."

"The tee ladies," repeated Angus. "The women's course committee. They set the rules."

"Is that not unusual?"

"Not for us," replied Alistair. "Been that way since the ladies of Kilcladdich and Kildrummy first established the course, as a comparatively peaceful means for settling differences."

"Such as upriver water access and choice peat moss."

"An excellent example," said Angus.

"It is, isn't it," I agreed. "And you say that your catalogue includes a selection of match reports. You don't have something in a milestone meet from 1767, do you?"

"Aye."

"I'll have that, too, I believe, and a long Kildrummy '20."

My selections were clumped onto the bar in a cloud of cumulative pub ambience. I gathered them up.

"Sorry, Mister Boisjoly," said Angus. "The rules must only be consulted on the premises."

"My room is on the premises," I pointed out.

"Aye, that's true." Angus leaned on a chair that he'd been putting right, and massaged his chin. Alistair performed a similar service for his own chin behind the bar.

"I'll take good care of them." I worked my way towards the stairs. "And I promise not to finish the crosswords."

"Hullo Anty." Tannin opened her door with a glass of whisky in her hand. "Got one already, thanks. What else are you selling?"

"A full set of Glen Glennegie golf course rules." I held up the exhibits. "And a blow-by-blow match report, circa 1767."

"You think something in there might have bearing on our current line of enquiry?" Tannin retreated into her room and I followed.

Tannin's room was like mine — woody and stony and starkly furnished with gently cracked pews and delicately imbalanced armchairs that tick-tock almost of their own accord.

"You never know which nuance or nicety might prove pertinent." I assumed a gentlemanly distance on a bench by the window, employing the sill as a quite serviceable bar top. The window, like mine, gave out onto the bog behind the pub and the watershed inland hills in the distance. "I'll take Kildrummy '04 — the last time the rules were changed for the last nine holes." I handed Tannin the other notebook. "You have the Kilcladdich '05. Try not to tear out any pages or doodle in the margins — I've given my word of care for these books."

"What are we looking for?" Tannin sat at her writing desk with her Kilcladdich '05 and her other Kilcladdich '05.

"Oh, peculiarities. Precedents. Pointlessly petty particularities." I thumbed open my Kildrummy '04. "For instance, in Kilcladdich, what are your options should your ball become 'fouled by a firm or unyielding filth'?"

"Ehm…" Tannin followed an index to page three. "None. You have to play the ball, regardless of its state of 'muck, mud, mire, or unsightly adherences'. You can't pick up the ball, even and especially to clean it."

"Whereas in Kildrummy, you have to," I noted. "A rule clearly written to offend the Kilcladdich side."

"What makes you say that?"

"The wording. *The player must pick up and clean any ball which has become fouled by a firm or unyielding filth, or the corrupting clay of Kilcladdich.*' It's subtle, but it's there if you look for it."

Tannin idly turned the pages and sipped her drink. "Here's one along similar lines — what happens 'should an honest strike be distrayed'?"

"By beast, imbecile, or feeble-minded child?" I asked, recalling my earlier encounter with this stipulation.

"Among other things," said Tannin. "The 1905 version adds '...or deceitful MacAngus'."

"Doubtless in response to this Kildrummy 1904 update which appends '...willfully wicked acts of villainy, such as those of a MacAlistair'. And the player has the option of horsewhipping the offending party or claiming a two-stroke allowance."

"In Kilcladdich it's a leather strop or retaking the hole." Tannin looked up from her rule book. "Do you think this case is going to turn out to be about golf?"

"I had a second uncle who thought that everything is, or at least that it should be," I said. "He used to tell me, 'Andy...' he thought my name was Andy... 'Never marry a woman until you've partnered her in a mixed open.'"

"He lived by that?"

"And died by it," I recalled. "Ended his days a bachelor. And, it turns out, a thirty-two handicap. I think the theory was that any woman who could carry him over eighteen holes would put up with anything."

"He wasn't murdered though, your uncle," supposed Tannin.

"No," I said. "Heart attack. Got a fluke hole-in-one on the sixteenth at Hendon. Died of shock on the spot."

"So, possibly not relevant to the death of Lummy MacAlistair."

"Only in that both tragedies go back, as does everything if you subscribe to Uncle Elmer's world view, to golf."

"You mean the match that started the feud."

"The match that entrenched the feud, if it's not being pedantic," I clarified. "There was already considerable competition for choice access to resources. This game…" I held up the match report. "…merely formalised a casual, freestyle acrimony, in large part owing to mutual accusations of cheating."

"You think one side or the other might have a legitimate complaint?"

"Let's have a look…" I set the Kildrummy rules on the window sill and opened the withered match report on my lap. "Quite a cast. In addition to the players, Duff MacAlistair and Lachlan MacAngus, there was an arbiter for Kilcladdich and one for Kildrummy, caddies, fore-caddies, observers, one scribe, one falconer, and four time-keepers, courtesy of Glen Glennegie Parish Church. I wonder how the church enters into things."

"Right here." Tannin put her finger on a page, and read, "'Any player who has lost his ball is penalised one stroke, and must re-tee from where the ball was last seen, if the player cannot recover it before the time-keepers have completed two renditions of The Bonnie Lass o' Fyvie (sad version).' I think the time-keepers are the church choir."

"That explains this," I read from the match report; "'In consultation with his caddie, which nearly lasts the fully allowed three choruses of Brochan Lom, Mister MacAngus selects his iron niblick for the purpose of thrashing a water vole. The water vole out-distances Mister MacAngus by thirty yards over the seventh fairway.'"

"Certainly jollier than a stopwatch," observed Tannin.

"Isn't it?" I agreed. "We have a similar system at the Juniper — statute nine, subsection four of the catering committee rulebook, says that a bottle of champagne shall be deemed to have been downed in one if it's uncorked and emptied by a single member after the beginning and before the end of God Save the King."

"That sounds like just a waste of champagne," opined Tannin.

"Well, exactly, which is why the rule was clarified to include all three verses and, in the case of a magnum or Lambrusco, the fourth unofficial verse. Sadly, this revision wasn't widely shared before New Year's, and several members were hospitalised."

"Alcohol poisoning?"

"Laryngitis."

Tannin gazed at me, as though contemplating the value of pursuing the theme, and then returned her attention to her Kilcladdich book of regulations. "I get the impression that these rules are contrary purely to be contrary."

"Probably that's the case today, but at the time I expect the intention was to gain advantage." I referred once again to the match report; "'At the eleventh tee, Mister MacAngus calls for a judgement on his opponent's ball, which he says is not that with which Mister MacAlistair started the match. Mister MacAlistair is judged to have employed a replacement after Friar Murdo Broon, having been struck by Mister MacAlistair's ball in The Bunker of Deep Sighs, keeps it.'"

"But according to the Kilcladdich rules..." Tannin flipped back one page. "...that's allowed."

"It's allowed to change your ball in Kilcladdich," I agreed, "but in Kildrummy it's forbidden to finish the game with a different ball to that with which you started."

"Hence the accusations of cheating."

"Precisely," I said. "I see here, for instance, that on the ninth hole, MacAngus is stymied by MacAlistair. It's important to note that the ninth hole is on Moan Innes, which is neutral ground, and players are subject to their respective clubhouse rules."

"That's absurd," noticed Tannin.

"It gets absurder... 'Mister MacAlistair argues that his ball was governed by Kilcladdich rules, and must not be moved, and Mister MacAngus contends that he is entitled to move the ball, according to Kildrummy rules.'"

"What was decided?"

"It doesn't say..." I searched both sides of the page.

"Who won the match, then?"

"It doesn't say that, either," I reported. "They probably just flipped a coin."

"And then argued about it for a hundred and fifty years," marvelled Tannin.

"Because it's insoluble," I said. "From the perspective of one side of the river, the other side cheated and, in fact, they did. And it's equally true that neither side cheated."

"My father used to say that Glen Glennegie was the most challenging course he ever played," reminisced Tannin. "He had me pack him a dozen spare niblicks — he knew once he'd broken all of them, it was time to quit for the day."

"Ahoy!" Tannin didn't say that and, obviously, I knew that I hadn't, and the unexpected nature and tone of 'Ahoy' when a chap's reflecting on a hundred and fifty years of misunderstandings, obstinate or otherwise, is unsettling. I think that I was reaching for my drink in the moment, and in my agitation I managed to push it out the window. I'd been in this exact same situation before, though, and my reflexes are honed and heightened, like those of a panther in a crowded pub during a close-fought darts derby. I leapt from my bench and caught the glass even as it fell, however I also knocked the book of Kildrummy rules off the sill.

I leaned out and watched the book fall, fluttering like an immature and inept fledgling, straight down and into the rain barrel.

"Ahoy." Isabette, who had been standing with Ludio beneath my room, one window over, now regarded me with short impatience. "What did you want to do that for?"

"My reasons are my own," I replied. "You only need to know that I have them, and they are sound. Fish that out for me, won't you Ludio?"

"Right oh, Anty." Ludio dashed over to the rain barrel and applied what emergency rescue techniques he knew.

"And what do you want, young firebrand, calling out 'ahoy' without any warning?" I asked Isabette.

"Ahoy is a warning, Anty," countered Isabette. "I wanted to get your attention."

"You couldn't just knock on my door?"

"You're not home."

"Clearly you didn't know that."

"Well, that's just it, Anty, I couldn't just knock on your door — Angus and Alistair wouldn't let me go up to your room alone."

"Why do you want to go up to my room at all?"

"To be alone."

"I see."

"With Ludio."

"Ah," I surmised. "I think not, Isabette. Neither I nor my room shall be a party to anything that could give your mother justification to strike me with a scone. Hold hands in church, like we had to do."

"It's not like that, Anty — we just want a little privacy."

"To swoon, to moon, to in love's fair boon delight in your room," elaborated Ludio.

"Yes. That," agreed Isabette dubiously. "I'll say I'm coming up to visit Miss Tibbits, and a few minutes later Ludio pops up to see you to borrow a collar stud or some such boy thing. Then you can make yourself rare for a bit."

"Where am I supposed to go while you're in my room?"

"Oh, I don't know, Anty — where are you now?"

"Right, yes, fair point, well made, but negotiations remain, nevertheless, at an impasse."

"You want your book back or not?"

"I believe there's been a breakthrough."

"The door shall remain open," I dictated to Isabette and Ludio, "and Vickers, who has the ears of an owl, the eyesight of a hawk, and the moral latitude of an Augustinian convert to Calvinism, will be right outside. Isn't that so, Vickers?"

We waited for a moment in silence.

"He's lying in wait," I said. "Don't test him."

"You needn't worry, Anty," claimed Isabette. "We just need a bit of respite from the all-seeing eye of the regime."

"You could worry a little, Anty," corrected Ludio. "The heart most constant is the heart most ardent."

"No, he needn't worry at all, Ludio," countermanded Isabette.

"I'll just be next door, not worrying."

"Wee dram 'afore you go," urged Isabette.

"Anty's just said he has important business next door," pointed out Ludio.

"It's just nice to be among people who know about us, isn't it?" Isabette sat down on the bed and exhaled long relief. "Ludio — pop down and get us a bottle of something dangerous, will you, and three glasses."

"Oh, right oh." Ludio skulked out the door and — this becomes important in a moment — closed it behind him.

I set about offering convalescent care to the Kildrummy rules book. First, I inserted bits of notepaper between the pages and then pressed the book under a heavy trunk, on which I placed my bootbox, on which I sat. Isabette sat on the bed, swinging her legs like an eight-year-old on a pier.

"Oh, I say, Ludio's closed the door." I hopped up and opened the door wide, and there stood Yvaine MacAngus.

CHAPTER NINE

The Decidedly Dicey Dilemma of the Dictates of Discretion

Now, this was a bind. As a gentleman, I had to assure Yvaine that her daughter's presence in my room was entirely innocent, and as a gentleman of my word I could do no such thing. I had to choose my next words more carefully than I'd ever done.

"Gah!"

"Mister Boisjoly." Yvaine spoke in the flat, ambiguous monotone of the paid assassin or career librarian, and yet still managed to make my name sound like it would get her excommunicated. She added, "Isabette," as it might have been the second part of an equation; Boisjoly + Isabette = a mother's just wrath.

"What ho, Mrs MacAngus." I mentally searched the scrolls for some suitable balm but anything I could recall from the countless times I'd found myself in similar situations would have only made things worse, as they invariably did the countless times I'd found myself in similar situations. The best of the bleakest that came to me was a cloudy recollection of what Isabette herself had proposed, "Isabette's just come to borrow a collar stud."

Yvaine's blank, piercing gaze mollified into a sort of knowing, maternal smile which was somehow more terrifying, and she walked past me into the room.

"It's all fine, Mister Boisjoly. I know what's going on here."

"No, you don't."

"I was young once too, you know."

"No, you weren't. I mean to say, of course you were. Still are. Fine figure of a woman."

Yvaine raised a hand with a gentle, calm-down sort of motion, and I reflexively ducked.

"It's perfectly all right. I know that you're a gentleman, and would never dally with a lady's reputation."

"Quite right," I readily agreed. "I don't dally. Not a dallying bone in my body."

"Nevertheless." Yvaine assumed a worryingly cheerful, mock gravity. "There'll be no more unchaperoned interviews in your private rooms."

"No, no. Indeed, even this one is the result of an innocent misunderstanding." The blood was returning to my extremities, now, and my evasion gland was once again sending instructions. "You see, I thought this was my room."

"Isn't it?"

"It's Miss Tibbits'," I claimed. "They're very similar. And, now I think of it, I have that very same bootbox. Isabette was visiting Miss Tibbits, I believe, and I — once again, believing this to be my room and quite empty — entered. Innocently. I entered innocently."

"And then closed the door."

"As one does after entering a room one supposes to be one's own. And then when I reopened it, there you were."

Yvaine levelled a diagnostic squint on me, and I fancy that she might have been leaning toward a reluctant credulity, had Ludovic not at that very moment turned up at the door with a bottle and three glasses in hand. That much was all right, or it might have been, but for what happened next.

"Oh, hello." Ludovic made this neutral statement, and all was diplomatic deadlock, until Tannin appeared and came, she doubtless thought, to the rescue.

"What ho, Ludio." She threaded her arm through his. "Anty, Isabette, Mrs MacAngus. Ludio and I are just having a quick one in my room, aren't we Ludio?"

"Oh, yes, that's right."

"Let's go, Ludio."

"Right. So long."

"Cheerio."

And the pair of vandals, having done their worst, tripped merrily along the corridor to Tannin's room.

"As I was saying..." Yvaine regarded me beneath hooded eyes, her arms crossed before her. "...there'll be no more private interviews until the formalities are seen to."

"Formalities?"

"Off you go, Isabette," Yvaine instructed her daughter, and Isabette left the room in what I felt was inadequately low spirits. If anything there was an impish skip to her step.

"You should know, Mister Boisjoly, that Isabette's uncle doesn't think a great deal of you." Yvaine imbued a dangerous depth of meaning to her words, like Lady Macbeth, just without the redemption arc.

"I know. Thinks I'm a lace-lined pan-loafy. I mean to say, really, pan-loafy, fair enough..."

"It's not going to be a problem." Yvaine spoke in hushed tones and, with a heretofore hidden talent for irony, pushed the door closed. "You can get round him easily enough."

"I appreciate your confidence, but it's a difficult charge to answer. I'm not entirely sure what it means."

"You need to tell him that you're going to vote for Kildrummy at the tasting."

"I beg your pardon." I spoke coolly. "Are you suggesting that I should betray my solemn — belay that — my sacred duty of blind neutrality to the Glen Glennegie jury, just to gain favour with Isabette's uncle?"

"No, Mister Boisjoly." Yvaine moved toward the window or, more likely, away from the door. "On the contrary — you only need to *tell* Duncan that he's got your vote, and then, to avoid any appearance of impropriety, you vote for Kilcladdich."

"You want me to vote for Kilcladdich."

"I do."

"Why?"

"Why, for your own good sake, Mister Boisjoly," alleged Yvaine. "You can't be seen to be favouring the MacAngus distillery, now, can you?"

"So, I avoid the appearance of favouritism to Kildrummy, if I'm following your line of reasoning, by showing favouritism to Kilcladdich."

"That's right."

"But that will put your own distillery at a disadvantage."

"Can't be helped. It's for the greater good."

"I see. Right oh. If I may, though, the greater good of what?"

"It's the only way that Duncan will give his blessing."

"Still not quite there, yet, Mrs MacA. Is this blessing of his something that I especially want?" I asked, not without a trace of pride. "He thinks I'm a pan-loafy, of the particularly noxious lace-lined variety."

"I'll talk to Duncan, then," concluded Yvaine. "I'll assure him that you'll be voting Kildrummy at the tasting. You just make sure that you vote Kilcladdich. Then everything will be all set."

"All set?" I queried. "All set for what?"

"Obviously, Mister Boisjoly…" Yvaine spoke now at an open, indeed, dangerously performative volume, and in fact opened the door. "…your marriage to my daughter."

"For never was a story of more woe, than brought on by Isabette and her Ludio." I spoke this trenchant paraphrase as I joined the star-crossed lovers at their table in the otherwise deserted Mash and Mashie bar room. "Do you know what sort of woe you've landed me in?"

"You didn't tell Mama about us, did you?" asked Isabette.

"No, I didn't tell Mama about you," I replied with meaning. "Although there was a moment when I was gravely tempted. I believe it was about the time that our engagement was announced. Do you like a large family, by the way? I should have asked before now, but what with everything and whatnot…"

"I assumed you'd given us up." Isabette dribbled whisky into my glass.

"Oh, thank you very much," I said with that subtle trace of irony for which I'm so well regarded. "I hope I've finally earned your confidence — trust is one of the pillars of a good marriage, I believe, along with financial stability and not reading a chap's love letters out loud in church."

"Sorry, Anty, but you did tell Constable Budge about Molly and the new vicar."

"No, I didn't."

"You didn't?"

"That was Lummy," I straight-set the record. "I merely fell on my sword when Constable Budge chose to repeat it in open court."

"I'm sure if he did, he had a very good reason." Isabette spoke with a worryingly admiring tone for a girl in love with Ludovic and, technically, engaged to me. "He's very clever. They made him a detective sergeant, you know."

"This was a younger, starry-eyed Constable Budge, eager to win the favour of the court with an amusing anecdote," I acknowledged. "Nevertheless, not tremendously sporting of him, I think we can agree. Not a patch on your poetry recital, but not an example to be emulated by the nation's youth, either. No, the only stalwart in that whole, sordid affair, turns out to be the same chap who's even now drinking your whisky and keeping your secret. Pass me that water pitcher, will you, Ludio?"

Ludio, as it happens, was staring intently at that same water pitcher, as though he saw in it foreboding shadows of the future.

"Why didn't you tell Mrs MacAngus about us, Anty?"

"Because I gave my word I wouldn't, Ludio," I explained that which should not need explaining.

"Right. Your word. You're a man of honour, and all that." Ludio slid the pitcher across the table. "And now you're honour-bound to marry Isabette. You worked that a treat, I'll give you that."

"I did, rather, didn't I?" I added a sardonic spot of water to my whisky. "Maybe it was meant to be — what do you say, Bettes old thing? Shall we seize the risk of marital bliss? Or hazard destiny's paths alone, accompanied only by the shadow of what might have been; me to send an anonymous white rose once a year on that which would have been our wedding day, you to wonder from whence it came, and to stiffen with a frisson of melancholy whenever you hear the haunting refrain of *When A Fellow's On The Level With A Girl That's On The Square?*"

"I knew it." Ludio tried to slam down his glass dramatically, but instead just spilt a bit.

"He's joking, Ludio."

"You see?" I pointed out. "We're clearly soul mates. Most people just think I'm babbling."

"I still think that. What did Mama say to you after I left?"

"Oh, the usual words of advice from a woman of years and experience to a future son-in-law," I filtered. "She advised me to learn to truly appreciate burnt eggs, and to never cross your putting line wearing spikes."

"Sound advice."

"Here's some more — you'll want to be cautious about keeping secrets, you two." I took a paternal sip of my whisky. "You don't want to end up like Coals Stokely."

"Who is Coals Stokely?" asked Ludovic.

"I'm glad you asked, Ludio, because I was about to tell you regardless. Coals Stokely is a member of my club and a lonely-hearted martyr to love. Last year he met by chance a girl by the name of Lenore Bambury. Pretty girl, solid, honest, and in line to inherit half her father's substantial railway holdings. Coals was smitten, but Coals was also a prize-winning poltroon. Sort of chap who'd claim he didn't drink cocktails — and stand by it — rather than wave for a waiter."

"We understand, Anty," exhaled Isabette. "He was of a nervous disposition."

"Well put. Very nervous. He was once required to give evidence in court regarding a minor traffic infraction to which he'd been witness," I recounted. "Pled guilty to the crime himself and paid the fine, rather than perform for the gallery. So, what does a chap like that do when he's madly in love with a girl?"

"Bucks up?"

"Hardly," I said. "No, he strategizes. You see, among the Juniper membership is Hollers Holloway, who was keeping company with Lenore's sister, Bobbi. In fact there was an understanding."

"They were engaged," translated Ludovic.

"They were very engaged. The Bishop of Winchester himself was reportedly the dark-horse tenor of record for an imminent third reading of the banns."

"So Coals got Hollers to get Bobbi to argue his case to her sister," supposed Isabette.

"Indirectly, yes," I said. "You see, Hollers was widely known for his uninhibited approach to the keeping of confidences — tell anyone anything, so long as it was a secret. If you asked him his name he'd rebuff you like the family silver, but tell him you're clandestinely seeking the guidance of a noted nerve specialist for your Sunday morning absinthe habit, and he'll be stopping strangers on the street to share the news."

"Why would anyone tell him anything private, then?" asked Isabette.

"Few do. He was out of the local news cycle before he was twelve. He ran so short of secrets to tell that once, at Eton, he grassed himself up for smuggling a white mouse into Latin class. He found the substitute wanting but, what else could he do? No one would trust him with anything, so he took to smuggling white mice into all his classes and snitching on himself during attendance check. The administration of poor Holler's transgressions became so onerous that eventually Eton introduced a rule permitting one white mouse per boy, per term."

"Not the sort of chap you want to trust with a delicate mission of romance, then," opined Ludovic. "

"The precise opposite of Coals' line of thinking," I differed. "After swearing Hollers to secrecy, he confides that he's absolutely hatters for Lenore; those eyes, those lips, those shapely etc.

This carries on for a while, Coals affecting to enjoy Hollers' company so that he can justify standing him a couple of deep ones most evenings at the club. I overheard one of these conferences — Coals has no talent for subtlety, and would say things like 'I say, this is a ripe, round, devilishly attractive vintage, isn't it? Don't tell her I said this, but it rather puts one in mind of Lenore Bambury, don't you think?'"

"So, what happened?" asked Ludovic.

"Nothing at all," I announced to marvelling ears. "Weeks go by, and Lenore Bambury remains a mere nodding acquaintance, at best. Coals even mustered the courage to conspire to happen upon Lenore at the intermission bar of the Criterion. She'd forgotten his name. Thought it was Embers."

"Awfully near — Coals, Embers," said Ludovic in her defence.

"In fact his real name is Stephen."

"Oh, right," said Ludovic. "Of course."

"Which rankled all the more, because of course he assumed that his plan was working, at least insofar as Hollers was faithfully betraying his confidence. But what he didn't know was that, for the first time in his life, Hollers was keeping mum."

"But, why?" asked Ludovic, who was clearly taking mental notes.

"It turns out that Hollers had received the lesson of a lifetime when he told his mother, who co-chaired the Ladies' Abstention Convention with Lenore and Bobbi's mother, that Bobbi had entered herself for the Stratford to Ealing Tavern Trail Endurance Marathon — first prize, a silver chalice that would be honoured for infinite refills for a year at all participating pubs. She was in with a chance, too, but when her mother learned of it she whisked Bobbi off to summer with a maiden aunt in Shrewsbury. She barely had time to return Hollers' letters and gifts, never mind set fire to them first and push them through his letterbox."

Ludovic dropped his forehead to his hand, and raised the other in an 'enough' motion. *"Two departed, in silence and tears. Half broken-hearted, to sever for years.* End the tale here, Anty, I can take no more."

"Well, I want to know how it ends," said Isabette. "What became of Coals?"

"He certainly learned his lesson, too, I can tell you that much," I reported. "Speaks up when he feels something wants saying, and often when it doesn't especially. He stopped by my table last week to tell me he didn't care for the way I took butter directly from the dish, and that I should end what he assumed was a wholly sentimental attachment to my current barber."

"What about Hollers?"

"Happily married, now."

"She came back to him?" Ludovic raised a smiling, hopeful, soon-to-be-disappointed face.

"No, not at all," I said. "No, they still don't speak, which I expect is awkward, because after listening to Coals' exhaustive inventory of her beauty, intelligence, character, and spirit, Hollers proposed to Lenore."

"Perhaps Anty's right." Ludovic turned a hard, earnest pout on Isabette. "After all, this can't go on forever."

"No, I know."

"We could run away," suggested Ludovic, then to me he added, "Isabette has always dreamed of living in a university town."

"Anty doesn't need to hear about that, Ludio."

"Of course, it's just a dream," Ludovic assured me, "but Isabette will often open a word window on a Glasgow scene, through which we watch her live her dreams." He smiled at something. Presumably not his metric line. "She often jokes that she could go on ahead, and wait for me there indefinitely."

"I was going to ask about that, Ludio," I remembered a handy shift in subject, "I understand that you have no wish to pursue the role of master distiller."

Ludovic held up his glass and affected to examine it from various angles.

"There has been some doubt expressed regarding my aptitude for certain aspects of the trade. And I confess that in the past the mechanics, patience, and irksome attention to every infinitesimal detail, have often eluded me. It doesn't help that methanol and ethanol are such similar words, either, and do they really, I mean really and truly, care about a couple of degrees Fahrenheit, one way or the other?"

"I think it's a matter of physics," I said.

"Did you know that methanol was poisonous?" asked Ludovic in that way one does when one is seeking an ally.

"I think it's widely understood, yes."

"Well, I maintain that opinion was predisposed against me," complained Ludovic with the cool, detached whinge of the unjustly persecuted. "Even before we had to redistill a thousand gallons of wort."

"Ten thousand, Ludio," reminded Isabette.

"You see?" pounced Ludovic. "It's all minutia."

With instructions that Ludovic should linger and entertain me with a sonnet he was working on, Isabette left us. A few minutes later, Ludovic bade me, "Farewell, dear rival on the tilting fields of yearning," and took himself off.

I brooded for a while on life and death and the subtle undertones of rosehip evident in the younger Kilcladdichs, until Vickers came down the stairs and reminded me of something important.

"Good afternoon, sir. Have you lunched yet, today?"

"I'm not sure..." I ruminated on the point with a sip of whisky. "Have I?"

"I believe not." Vickers cast a pie-seeking eye over the bar. "I find that when gentlemen are participating in whisky and wine juries they will sometimes overlook certain fundamentals. If you'll recall our trip to Loire last year to cast your vote in the *Goutte d'Or*, you forgot to sleep for three nights in a row."

"I did not forget to sleep, Vickers," I reminded him. "I forgot how."

"Nevertheless, if you haven't eaten since breakfast, it's wise to dilute the whisky with something other than rainwater."

"Actually, now I think of it, I did have a concrete shortbread. That should hold me for a bit — it's going to take days before my body even begins to break that down... Great Scottish science, Vickers! They were tough enough, but it wouldn't take an axe to split them!"

"No, sir? I'm very gratified to…"

"No, I mean to say… there's going to be another murder!"

"I don't follow."

"Then I'll dash on ahead. If Budge returns here, send him to the Kildrummy distillery."

It was all the sheep could do to keep up, and indeed the herd had spread itself into a thin line between an older, more retiring rear guard and a spritely youth contingent by the time we were crossing Glen Glennegie bridge.

The distillery was fine. It was calm and quiet and cooking away, with jolly great plumes of white fumes issuing from the chimney and, for that matter, from every fissure and split. The wind was slow and heavy with peaty perfume. There was, in short, an unquantifiable and yet undeniable shushability about everything — exactly like that period after a vicar has shown his slides of his visit to the Holy Land and he's opened the floor to questions.

And then the distillery blew up.

CHAPTER TEN

The Boisjoly Withdrawal from Kwazulu-Natal

"Have you ever seen a distillery explosion, Vickers?"

"Yes, sir." Vickers brought us each a tall whisky and whisper to a table by the fireplace. "I was batman to your grandfather during the British withdrawal from Kwazulu-Natal. He was in charge of destroying all materiel of strategic value that could not be evacuated."

"Spiking the big guns, that sort of thing?"

"This, I expect, is what was intended by the order." Vickers added a matronly pour of rainwater to my whisky. "But your grandfather's notion of strategic value did not align, precisely, with that of Brigade Command."

"He focused, I'm guessing, on preventing the distilleries from falling into enemy hands."

"With tears in his eyes," recalled Vickers. "It was the most composed and courageous I'd seen him throughout the war."

"Any idea how he did it?"

"Flares, sir," replied Vickers. "I would open the valves of the condensers and set the temperature. Then, as the methanol overflowed your grandfather would shoot a signal flare into the liquid which, as you know, is highly volatile."

"Efficient."

"In the main, yes, although your grandfather's aim could be erratic."

"Lavishly toasted the fallen, did he?"

"He felt that was the only way to honour them," said Vickers, his eyes downcast. "And he wanted to avoid leaving behind any spirits that might give aid and comfort to the enemy."

"Well, assuming the same technique was employed just now in Kildrummy, the killer's aim was true," I said. "Blew the roof right off the building — for a moment, at least. It hopped up, and then plopped right back down again. Put me in mind of my Uncle Horace's regrettable interest in steeplechasing prior to the invention of a truly effective toupée glue. The door shot off, too, as though out of a cannon. Had I not ducked, in fact, you'd be this very minute undertaking the sad and, I think we can agree, ultimately futile task of trying to replace me."

"I take it there was nothing that could be done for Mister MacAngus."

"Unless you count a warm and well-enunciated but largely fictional eulogy, I'm afraid not. I checked."

"You were gone only some twenty minutes, sir."

"There wasn't a great deal to check, Vickers." I calmed my recollections with a steadying whiskler. "Budge was quite right — the fire burned itself out straight away. Indeed, the explosion had such puff that it suffocated the flames and very nearly extinguished the peat furnace. By the time the ad-hoc fire brigade returned from the seas where, to a man, they'd been fishing, it was all over but for a positively titanic housekeeping bill."

"And we're quite certain that it was intentional."

"That, or the most uncanny coincidence since Stucco Somersby and I both attended Cynthia Hannibal-Poole's national election fancy-dress sun-upper dressed as Lord Curzon," I said, stretching an analogy. "And even then Stucco thought he was wearing a Humpty-Dumpty costume."

"Has Mister Budge reached any conclusions?"

"I left him sifting the ashes," I said. "Doubtless he'll be along presently, though — he seemed anxious for a meeting of minds when you told him that I'd predicted a second murder. I think he assumes I did it."

"I fail to see how," spoke Vickers in reflexive defence.

"No, well, you wouldn't, would you?" I replied. "You don't have Budge's keen instinct for demographics. I'm from London, you see. I expect the only vexing obstacle to a conviction, in his view, is that when the first murder occurred I was on a train among unimpeachable witnesses."

With that helpful cue, Tannin stepped down the stairs, and the door of the pub burst open in that way doors will burst open when staggered into. Budge leaned on the door frame and coughed a cloud of dust into the room. He stumbled in, still wheezing, and took off his greatcoat, creating a solid personal atmosphere of smoke and smoulder and smell of wet and well-worn wool.

"What ho, Badger. Tally ho, Tannin." I held up my drink, to help them find their way. "Something for the dusty trail?"

"I daren't." Budge coughed again and shuffled to my table. "On duty." He saddled an adjacent chair with his coat and fell into another.

"The law-abiding public needs you at your biassed best, Detective Sergeant," Tannin reminded him as she took possession of the facing fireplace chair.

"Fair to say it's your duty, Budgler," I continued, "to take a medicinal measure with warm water. Vickers, if you'll play nurse — the Kildrummy '09s are acclaimed for their throat-clearing properties, owing to the introduction of a brace of burnt-oak *Viina* casks from Finland."

"Your man tells me that you knew the distillery was going to blow up," commented Budge.

"I don't recall you mentioning that in the detective club meeting minutes," complained Tannin.

"Time was at a premium," I explained. "I only recalled some twenty minutes ago that Duncan had asked for his axe. He had no call for an axe, unless he was going to perform significant renovations to his still, which has not been materially altered in seventy years."

"Assuming that's what he wanted the axe for, what does that tell you?" asked Tannin.

"That he knew — or at the very least, he thought he knew — the secret process."

"Aerating the methanol before redistilling it, and exposing it directly to peat smoke," coughed Budge.

"Precisely. And, as you've no doubt also concluded, this is the same incandescently dangerous procedure that Lummy MacAlistair was performing when he, too, was reduced to his constituent parts." Then I added, "Thank you, Vickers," for he had returned from the bar with a tray and three fresh vials of insight. "Did you find a flare?"

Budge didn't answer straight away. He was looking at his whisky like a beloved stuffed bear that he'd assumed lost to the years. He took up the glass and breathed in its atmosphere and then trickled a tantalising taste onto his tongue.

He put down his glass and then dove into the folds of his greatcoat. When he returned he placed the charred and swollen remains of a burnt flare on the tray.

"And, just as you say, there was also a crude hole in the floor to the peat furnace," Budge added. "Fancy both distillers working out the secret process at the same time."

"Clearly, Budgets, they didn't," I said. "This is what struck me about this whole affair from the outset, and now doubly so — the extraordinary timing."

"I noticed that myself." Budge nodded knowingly at his whisky. "As soon as the Londoners get here, things start blowing up."

"There's that, yes. Shrewdly observed." I toasted the point with a sardonic sip of subtle-sap. "But there's also the notable concurrence of two distillers independently rediscovering the same secret which has remained hidden to everyone for a hundred and fifty years, and then for both of them to be killed by that very secret, days apart."

Budge drank luxuriously, with his eyes closed. His eyes opened with the inspiration of the barley.

"Someone told them."

"Someone told them," I agreed. "And what they were told was not the real process, if there even is such a thing."

"Why do you say that?"

"A lifelong weakness for the theatrical," I confessed. "But if it is the real process, it's a coincidence — that which was told to Lummy and Duncan was, in a very real and satisfyingly dramatic fashion, the murder weapon."

"These are master distillers, Mister Boisjoly," pointed out Budge. "They're not going to risk their lives and livelihoods chasing a fleeting, trace distinction."

"These are, above all, competing whisky-makers," I countered. "They're literally feuding. That's in addition to the Glen Glennegie jury, the winning of which guarantees ten years of prosperity. And don't underestimate the lengths a craftsman will go in the pursuit of perfection. Did you know that there are brotherhoods of monks in Belgium who, in order to achieve the absolutely precise balance of humidity, temperature, and yeast culture in the manufacture of their artisanal beers, actually live in Belgium?"

"So you think it comes down to peat smoke, then," concluded Budge.

"In a manner of speaking, yes," I said. "If that manner is the precise opposite. I think what it comes down to is largely irrelevant. Having said that, I would certainly like to know. I can't imagine it would have a bearing, but there's a legendary hundred-and-fifty-year-old case of whisky that, it is whispered under tables and in slurred tones, would give a very sturdy clue to the true secret process, assuming there is such a thing."

"Eh? A hundred-and-fifty-year-old case of whisky?"

"Apparently," I looked to Vickers, who was smiling at something. "Isn't that so, Vickers?"

"Sir?"

"The hundred-and-fifty-year-old case of Glen Glennegie."

"Oh, yes, sir."

"But you don't think it's pertinent, now," presumed Budge.

"I suppose it depends on what you mean by pertinent," I speculated. "It would certainly bring a great deal of meaning to my life, but this presupposes that the case exists and that it could be had for some reasonable price, say, unto half my kingdom."

"I'll put up the other half," offered Tannin.

Budge lost himself momentarily again in his whisky, and then coughed and blew his nose in light reflection.

"It's your view, then, that Lummy and Duncan were tricked into creating a volatile environment that could be, and indeed ultimately was, touched off with a flare."

"Consider the alternative, Budgers," I proposed. "They each of them independently stumbled upon the same, probably incorrect, technique for introducing peat smoke into the young distillate, and were implementing it the very moment that someone randomly or accidentally — but certainly clandestinely — shot a signal flare into their distilleries. The odds of that couldn't be worse if I were betting on it to place at Ascot."

"Convincing enough, I'll admit." Budge took the edge off the admission with the rest of his whisky. "It doesn't change the fundamentals, though."

"No, I don't suppose it does," I agreed. "I say, Vickers, I sense the Detective Sergeant isn't quite out of the woods yet. Would you organise another drop of throat balm?"

"Perhaps just the one more," wheezed Budge. "Yes, regardless of how the killings may or may not have been done, it still all comes down to rote police work — I need to establish to the satisfaction of the Advocate Depute — much like your King's Counsel in England, just more professional — that Shelby Sheercliffe not only had the means and opportunity, but the motive to kill both men. If you have any ideas in that regard, they would be most welcome."

"I'll put my mind to it," I assured him. "Actually, I believe I have a thought on the subject already — she might not have done it. Outside rail, I realise, but I find it's often of value to look at these things from all angles."

"I take your point... ah, thank you, Mister Vickers... you think we should consider that someone else might have done in Duncan MacAngus." Budge nodded thoughtfully at this, sipped dreamily on his whisky, and then added, "Although take note, Mister Boisjoly, that puts you back in the picture."

"Tannin is from London, as well, by the way," I tattled.

"Actually I live in Richmond," corrected Tannin.

"Vickers still counts, though," I lowered my voice to confidential tones. "Rumour has it he has a veeery posh address in Kensington."

"Him too, then. Sorry, Mister Vickers."

"Things without all remedy should be without regard," quoth Vickers, with forbearance.

"So true," I mused. "So very true. Well, then, Budgerigar, what's the next step in the rote police work list of rainy-day activities?"

"I'll be wanting to establish the whereabouts of all possible suspects at the time of the explosion."

"Does that include many or any who aren't from London?" I asked.

"Not a lot, no. Most of the population of both towns is either at sea or at the docks," reported Budge to his whisky glass. "The only remaining interested parties are Yvaine MacAngus, Molly MacAlistair, the two gentlemen behind the bar, you lot, Shelby Sheercliffe, and Isabette and Ludovic."

"Intriguing way of putting it, Budgers," I observed.

"Putting what?"

"Isabette and Ludovic," I replied. "It just strikes me odd that you should bunch them together like that at the end of your inventory."

"Oh, right, yes. Keenly noted, Mister Boisjoly." Budge cleared his throat as a pretext to another swallow of strain-remover. "I suppose I need to tell you, in the strictest confidence you understand, that Isabette MacAngus and Ludovic MacAlistair are sweethearts."

"Really?"

"Yes." Budge spoke with the resigned sympathy of the fellow also-ran. "Sorry to have to tell you, but I thought you ought to hear it sooner rather than too late. I know that you thought you were in with a chance."

"I did, rather," I said. "But when did you hear this, Budgers? I ask because she and I were engaged only earlier this afternoon."

"You're engaged?"

"Well, precisely," I paltered. "Who's to say? We were a few hours ago, but things perforce move more quickly on the bustling banks of Glen Glennegie. You must have observed how much shorter is the average expected lifespan here than in, say, Spey."

"She only mentioned it an hour or so ago," said Budge with indeterminable feeling. "Just before the explosion."

"Well, that settles it then." I finished my whisky in a swallow. "Alert the society pages, Vickers — Anty Boisjoly is once again entertaining offers."

"Very good, sir."

"You don't seem very put out by it." Budge spoke with the tone of a man who values highly that which another discards.

"Candidly, Budgit, I'm not," I confessed. "I wouldn't want this to go any further, but I suspect the girl to be inconstant."

"Yes." Budge frowned thoughtfully at his glass. "She is, isn't she?" He looked up with renewed hope. "This whole thing with Ludovic might not be so very deeply carved in marble."

"Wouldn't surprise me if it was over already," I said. "Do I understand you to say that you, yourself, are Isabette's alibi for the latest pyrotechnic demonstration?"

"Hm? Oh, yes, I suppose I was."

"Well, that narrows the field appreciably. Vickers was here at the Mash and Mashie, as you know, and a Boisjoly is *ipso facto* innocent — it's been generations since we blew anything up. Deliberately, of course I mean."

"It certainly helps to know who did the first murder." Budge spoke as though expressing the unanimous view of the committee. "Touching on that," Budge distributed a conspiratorial squint equally between Tannin and myself, "I won't say I don't appreciate your assistance in refining my theories, but when it comes time to arrest Mrs Sheercliffe, I trust you'll leave the official business to the officials."

"Of course. I know where my talents begin and interests end. Ask anyone at Scotland Yard, Detective Sergeant Budge, and they'll tell you they've never heard of me," I assured him. "Some will be quite adamant about it, in fact."

"It's not a matter of credit, as such, you understand," explained Budge. "It's just, you see, some lads have it just handed to them, don't they — gilt birthright, no accountability their whole lives, nannies, best schools…"

"I know just the sort of jammy wodge you mean," I sympathised. "Chap I knew at Eton — knock-kneed, cross-eyed, and a snitch of the lowest order — just last year, without so much as opening the scheme to public tender, they made him Duke of Gloucester. It's not what you know but who you know, what?"

"Yes, just so," said Budge tentatively. "Chap like me, though, no real education to speak of, no funds to get one, either. Now, if a chap like that wants to move up in the police, when your chief inspectors have graduated law or what-have-you from Glasgow or Cambridge…"

"Say no more, Budging," I held up a desist hand. "Your meaning is as clear as a mountain stream that knows its own mind and isn't afraid to speak up. You want a nice, clean conviction, with no loose threads…"

"Exactly right."

"Even if it means arresting the wrong party."

"No."

"No? Doubtless I missed some nuance of your thinking. Would you care to start again?"

"I don't have time for all that, Mister Boisjoly." Budge swallowed the last of his whisky, meditated on the beauty of life for a moment, and then rose. "I've got an investigation to conduct." He hefted his greatcoat, which had now settled and dried into a sort of plaster cast, and fitted himself inside it. "Any idea where Mrs Sheercliffe can be found?"

"After the incident with the sheep, she retrieved her clubs and, I presume, went to the golf course," reported Vickers.

"Again?"

"Golfers are a breed apart," I said. "They will pursue their passion regardless the weather. I've seen some of them at it on even the nicest of days. Do you not putter?"

"Of course not. Who's got time for that nonsense. I suppose you do?"

"I do not." I shook my head sadly. "I have a condition."

Budge issued us each one curt, policeman's nod, and crunched out the door.

"A most determined young gentleman," adjudged Vickers.

"Determined to arrest Shelby Sheercliffe based on solid grounds to suspect her of being from London," elaborated Tannin.

"This was my distinct impression, Miss."

"You know what I must do now, don't you Tanners?"

"Two short ones?"

"Yes. And after that, we must solve these two murders before Budge thinks he has."

Vickers trayed two tidy tipples, and we toasted our respective health from a standing start. I, to take the temperature of two towns under siege of multiple, locked-room murders, and Tannin, to apply the same rigorous analysis to the Mash and Mashie, and all who sail in her.

"If I may, Mister Boisjoly," said Vickers as he helped me on with my coat. "I'm afraid there remains a rather vexing matter to be addressed."

"You mean, in addition to two locked-room murders."

"I do." Vickers assumed an expression, daintily balanced between embarrassed and discomfort, and withdrew an envelope from his pocket. "It's this letter, sir."

"Is it for me?"

"It's unaddressed."

"How do you come to have it in your pocket, then, Vickers?"

"This is the vexing matter to which I refer." Vickers ramped up the discomfort ratio. "I don't know."

"You don't know how it got into your pocket."

"Precisely, sir."

"That is vexing," I agreed. "What does it say?"

"I couldn't possibly open it, sir," said Vickers, aghast.

"No, quite right." I snipped the envelope out of his hand. "Good job I can." I withdrew the letter. "I doubt very much this is intended for me. Is there any chance you nicked it from Shelby Sheercliffe's room when you were there collecting golf balls?"

"This is as likely an explanation as any other," acknowledged Vickers. "Is there some indication of its origin?"

"Not even signed." I turned the letter over to confirm that diagnosis. "Which I suppose is to be expected, given the theme and subject matter."

"Is it…"

"Yes, Vickers, a poison pen." I recited as follows, *"Be fairly warned, Molly MacAlistair is not to be trusted. She's betrayed Lummy and she'll betray you and all, if you don't act first."*

CHAPTER ELEVEN

Anty Detects
a Dampening Effect

"Ya two-foot post in a three-foot hole, just like your brother you're a half-wit, but he got both halves," was the view that Angus was expressing to Alistair as they approached the pub, in front of which I was holding court with my sheep. Like Budge, they looked to be returning from a recently extinguished fire — they were muddy with damp dust and fatigued in the fashion of a hard job done well, and they were doing what they both loved best.

"Ach, ya cork anchor ya," volleyed back Alistair. "I'd say I've forgotten more about distilling than you ever knew, but the truth is that I've forgotten more about the native fauna of Papua New Guinea than you ever knew about distilling."

"Is that so, ya penn'orth of bad pennies?" enquired Angus. "Sadly for the Kildrummy distillery, though, believing fairy tales and trusting celestial omens is a pint short of a pint of expertise."

The men stopped as they reached the little lake of lambs.

"What are you doing here with all these sheep, Mister Boisjoly?" asked Alistair.

"Well, we *were* having a private conversation," I replied. "But in fact I'm glad you've come along. I take it that you've arrived from the scene of the most recent distillery renovation?"

"Aye."

"See anything unusual?"

"Aye," said Angus. "It's been blown up."

"Anything else, though building on that general theme?"

"That takes in a rather wide field, Mister Boisjoly," noted Alistair. "The door was gone, for example."

"I know," I reminisced. "Came at me with a distinctive top-spin, like one of those cheeky bowls Australian cricketers always seem to get away with. Where were you when it happened?"

"Kildrummy side," replied Angus.

"Coming back from the post," completed Alistair.

"And what did you see?"

"Not a thing." Alistair waded into the sheep, who followed our conversation like spectators absorbed in a game-making tennis rally. "We were too far. I'll tell you this, though, unlike Lummy, Duncan wasn't done cooking off the head when it happened."

"Yes, he was." Angus was also working his way toward the pub, but he elected a more circuitous route. Two sheep I'd come to call Muddy and Fuzzy cut him off. "He was just about to start distilling the heart."

"No, he wasn't," differed Alistair with the weariness of the repeated, unheard argument.

"How could you tell?" I asked.

"Smoke," answered Alistair. "There wasn't enough."

"Smell of methanol," differed Angus. "There was just enough."

"You must admit, though, Angus..." Alistair spoke as one delivering hard home truths. "...you have diminished faculties for such things." Alistair then addressed me in an aside. "I can tell you for a fact, Mister Boisjoly, that so dull is Angus' sense of taste and smell, that he's quite capable of drinking an entire glass of Kilcladdich without so much as a hiccough. I've seen it with my own eyes. It's impressive, in its own way — like a fire breather."

"Alistair, on the other hand, has a unique affinity for reading the signs," acknowledged Angus. "He's only got to stand outside for a mere ten minutes to know it's raining, and with a single glance at an impenetrable mist he can tell you it's foggy. I've seen him try to light his pipe no more than a dozen times in a row before declaring it windy."

"I understand that Detective Sergeant Budge found a flare in the wreckage," I diverted.

"Aye," said Angus. "Just like at Lummy's distillery."

"Where do you suppose it came from?" I asked. "I mean to say, obviously it came from a fishing boat, but would it have been missed? Would it not have been locked up?"

"It won't have come off a fishing boat," doubted Alistair.

"They wouldn't set out without their flares, and they all set out this morning," added Angus.

"It came from a golf bag," mystified Alistair while Angus, more mystifying still, nodded in agreement.

"A golf bag?" I repeated. "I'm not, to my eternal regret, a golfer, but I'm passingly familiar with the utensils — there are mashies and smashies and niblets and, I believe, balls, but I've never heard mention of signal flares. Is that a Scottish practice?"

"It's a Glen Glennegie practice," answered Alistair.

"How very festive. Reserved for milestone achievements, I assume — a birdie or a bunny or what have you."

"Every player carries a flare gun," said Alistair. "It's among the few common rules."

"And they're only meant to use them to call for help, should, say, a player be chipping out of a sand trap when the tide comes in," suggested Angus.

"Or crossing the river in a dory when the tide goes back out," added Alistair.

"Robert MacAngus pioneered the practice in 1852," recounted Angus, "when he sank to his knees in the Sludge Bunker between the beach and the twelfth fairway. Wrapped his ball in his garter flashes, soaked it in whisky and set it alight, then he hit the drive of his life — two hundred and twenty yards, onto the roof of the livery stable which, unfortunately, was made of thatch, but he got his point over, and clearly stated."

"It didn't enter the rules, though, until some twenty-five years ago," continued Alistair. "As recently as 1904, it wasn't uncommon for players, with no way to draw attention to their situation, to spend a cold and reflective night on Moan Innes."

"Or several days, in the winter," noted Angus.

"Or runoff season, of course, when the Glen Glennegie swells," reminisced Alistair, "and they were most likely to be swept out to sea." He gave me a happy, fatalistic smile. "The island quite often sinks altogether in runoff season."

"So, every golfer is required to carry a flare," I repeated for effect. "And they'd all know that, if they'd read the rules."

"At least one — per player, in good working order, by regulation," said Angus. "But it's a decision not to be taken lightly. Brodie MacAlistair learned that when he used his one flare to warn a foursome of Franciscan Hermits to let him play through on the fifth green. We'll never know for certain, but it's very likely he regretted that when he lost an oar on the way to Moan Innes. Last seen he was riding the prevailing current in the general direction of Norway."

"Iceland," dissented Alistair.

As they'd been speaking, the quibblers had navigated their respective paths through the throng, and were now very nearly at the door of the Mash and Mashie.

"By the way, Mister Boisjoly," recalled Angus, his hand on the door. "You'll be finished with those rules books by now, I expect."

"I still have need of them," I said distractedly. "They're vital to my investigations."

"Very well." Alistair spoke with slow reluctance. "You'll be sure to take care of them."

"Of course," I said with an offhand air. "My analysis is taking longer than expected, owing to legibility issues. Did you know that one of the books — Kildrummy, I believe it is — is a bit damp?"

"Damp?"

"Just a bit. Doubtless something to do with storage conditions behind the bar," I said. "I'm doing what I can for it, but I make no promises."

"That'll be Alistair's unconventional approach to the washing up," opined Angus. "He does do his best, though, the poor plonk."

"I expect it'll be down to the generous spirit with which Angus fills the water pitchers," suggested Alistair. "Very often, by accident or arrangement we shall never know, some water ends up in the pitchers."

I set out on my journey unhindered, at the outset, by the absence of a destination. I knew only that I needed to out-Holmes Budge who had started with the unearned twelve-stroke lead of a presumed culprit. I would have to re-interview the interested parties, wherever and whatever they might be hiding. In short, I required the fleetness of foot that studies show to be incompatible with shepherding.

There were two ways to get from Kilcladdich to Kildrummy. One was the bridge. The other way, in every possible manner in which it could be, was not.

Moving at a placid but purposeful pace, I entered the golf course at the first tee, crossed the third fairway, climbed the low but rocky grade that camouflages Stygian Rough from players approaching the fifth hole from the double dogleg, skirted Swampy Copse, the small wood of old-growth pine that almost completely surrounds the eighth tee, and descended the grassy meadow toward the edge of the Glen Glennegie river.

Here, this close to the river mouth, the rocky bank has descended from its height, where it's crossed by the bridge, to meet the end of the ninth fairway, which continues on Moan Innes. This end of the link is consequently lush and verdant, and the ideal spot on which to betray a flock of sheep, if a flock of sheep absolutely must be betrayed.

I had intended, drawing strength and inspiration from the morality tale that is Orpheus' ill-fated glance in the rear-view mirror, to simply row silently away without looking back. I stepped idly into the rowboat, taking the precaution to first say out loud "Well, I'm knackered, I'll just have a brief sit-down in this boat." I took up the oars and — I can see how Orpheus was caught out, now — heard an inquisitive "baaaa?"

It was the wide-eyed, shiny-eyed lamb I'd taken to calling Coyly, owing to his resemblance — not so much in physical appearance but in approach to interpersonal relations — to an unlicensed track tout of my acquaintance who would invariably draw on his infinite capacity for pathos when collecting — or, more often, pronouncing himself unable to pay out on — a wager. Coyly was gazing at me with those big, baleful orbs and I confess I very nearly lost my nerve when he took a tentative step onto the rocks, with a view to following me, but soon the fog closed over the bank, and the sheep became a bleating, echoing reminder that I was going to have to schedule some serious rallying and banter.

The river ran faster than expected. It was a very different experience to boating on the Serpentine, where one can simply row out to the centre and stop, lay out the picnic, recite a little poetry to the Penelope or Cynthia *du jour,* and rely on the currents to be about as tempestuous and troublesome as one would expect had the boat been parked on solid ground. As it was, I had to manoeuvre a bit upstream just to keep to a straight path to the other bank, and even then I bounced off the tip of Moan Innes.

Little harm comes from bouncing off the tip of an island like Moan Innes. It wasn't so much a body of land as a spongy, podgy accumulation of river sludge, overgrown, in the main, with bulrushes and cordgrass, but for a very rough circle in the very rough centre, which had been tamped down to form the famous ninth green/tenth tee ground. The divides which the river forms around the island take on very different personalities as they do so, and the current slowed appreciably as I pushed away with my oar towards the continent of Kildrummy.

My boat and I weaved and whirled and leed and swirled and in time bumped up against the little Kildrummy-side pier of mouldering wood and slime. Somewhere in the fog, Coyly whispered a faint forget-me-not.

The Kildrummy links are hilly and rocky where Kilcladdich is slippy and sloppy, and I soon regained my land legs as I climbed into and back out of Six Feet Under Deep Pot Bunker and its neighbouring rough, a three hundred-yard field of razor shale and irrigation issues called the Faery Garden. I circumvented the Valley of Quitters, a sand trap surrounding a column of rock at the centre of which is the par twenty-seven number thirteen, and soon enough I was at the coastal road where it meets the bridge. I was going to have just a little lie-down, but the grass was damp, and Molly was on the bridge, looking at something on the Kilcladdich side, her wrap of purple drapery flapping in the wind.

"What ho, the other Mrs MacA." I wobbled over and leaned on the parapet. "Still monitoring the demilitarised zone?" Molly and Ludovic had been on the bridge when I passed on the way to the distillery, and she had still been there when I returned to Kilcladdich.

"Where are you coming from?"

"Fourteenth fairway," I said. "I think I did quite well. Nearly lost a shoe in the seashell hazard, but I recovered on my short game, and here I am. You didn't send Ludio looking for me, did you?"

"He's down there." Molly gestured with her chin toward the ebbing mist which helpfully prevented my sheep from spotting me on high ground. "We were here waiting for a delivery of fertiliser, for the course... what's that lad doing now?"

"He appears to be moving in a south-easterly direction," I observed. "Or, put another way, he's coming here, looking slightly colicky. Is that contrary to expectations?"

"He's meant to be rowing half the lot over to the Kildrummy side."

"In the boat?" I asked, and Molly merely turned on me an unreadable regard.

"It's gone," called Ludovic as he achieved the road.

"Fancy that," I said. "You're looking dangerously French. Did you not do fire duty?"

Ludovic was decidedly dapper in riding britches and boots and a copper-coloured waistcoat with no jacket, notable when compared to Budge and the firefighting barmen, or to anyone charged with loading a half-portion of fertiliser into a boat.

"I was running the pumps, wasn't I?" Ludio seemed to characterise this as a grievance, as though it was the result of a failure to recognise his talents. "And at the time, the boat was on the other side of the river."

"Time and tide wait for no man," I pointed out, helpfully. "So, I conclude that you two can alibi each other for the time of the explosion."

"Alibi?" Molly spoke the word as a slur. "Who needs an alibi?"

"Not you," I assured her. "Nor Ludovic. You have each other."

"Ludio was taking barrows of fertiliser down Kilcladdich side," said Molly. "I was right here."

"Positioning you, very much like the omniscient voice in one of those German fables that always seem to feature a bridge, to alibi anyone who may have crossed here."

"What's all this about alibis?" Molly crossed her arms and, somehow, her eyebrows.

"It's a core concept in modern criminology," I explained. "Detective Sergeant Budge is taking a census of any that reside in the vicinity."

"He told me he'd worked out who did it," said Ludovic.

"A smoke screen," I said. "The man is operating on a different plain to you and me, investigatorially. He was telling me only an hour ago about his theory that we may be dealing with two separate killers."

"I only saw you," said Molly. "Then, after the explosion, Mister Budge and Angus and Alistair. Then the lot of you coming back."

"It's a start. I'll go ahead, then, and rule out the detective sergeant, the barmen, and self. Vickers, you'll be happy to hear, was already in the clear."

"Oh, and I saw Isabette." Molly accompanied this with a wholesale change in attitude, as though in that instant remembering that bunny-rabbits exist. "And her mother. I understand that you're due congratulations."

"Why, yes, and I'm delighted but not unsurprised that you heard about my unanimous election to head of the Juniper bunting committee all the way up here."

"She means your engagement to Isabette," said Ludovic, with trace undertones of citrus and sulphur."

"Oh, right, that too, of course," I said. "I finally broke her down."

"I'm very glad for you both." Molly beamed at me. Behind her, Ludovic did whatever the opposite of beaming is. Steaming, perhaps.

"Yes, congratulations, Anty." Ludovic's lips moved, but his jaw did not. "I hope there are no secrets or any such thing that might arise and prevent the nuptials."

"Isabette already knows about my brushes with the law," I acknowledged. "She finds it romantically roguish."

"Does she now?"

"She hasn't said as much, but I'm giving her the benefit of the doubt."

"Ludio." Molly spoke with iron goodwill — the same sort of cheery authority with which I expect Napoleon sent his brothers off to rule Spain and Italy. "Why don't you go and see if the boat's on the Kildrummy side?"

"Sound thinking," I said. "I'll bet that's a real possibility."

We watched Ludovic sulk down the hill and disappear into the limestone quarry that could make the difference between a scratch nine or an even eighty strokes on the eleventh hole.

"I gather you think there's something to this secret distillation process story." Molly walked to the inland side of the bridge, as though to create a buffer between us and the enquiring crowds.

"Only in the allegorical sense," I claimed. "Much in the same vein in which Sherlock Holmes took a view on the curious incident of the dog in the night."

"You don't think it's real, then." Molly gazed upriver, toward the watershed hills, overlapping and chasing each other off into a misty forever.

"My father thought so." I joined her at the parapet. "As did, I believe, Mister Tibbits and Mister Sheercliffe. They claimed to have tasted a pre-1767 Glen Glennegie."

"Do you believe it? They were half-looped half the time."

"They were fully looped, all the time," I corrected. "But my father's sensibilities were unaffected by drink, although now I come to say it, I'm not sure that theory was ever tested. In any case, he believed that there was some cardinal quality that was different to subsequent years."

"I expect you'd like to get a taste of that yourself," teased Molly.

"You have an uncanny sixth sense for the plainly obvious, Mrs MacAlistair."

"What if I told you that there really was a hundred-and-fifty-year-old case of Glen Glennegie?" Molly spoke into the wind, like a smuggler under a bridge. "And what if I went on to tell you that it still exists, and that I knew how you could get hold of it?"

"Frankly, I'm unsure," I admitted. "I have no real frame of reference. Once, when I was six years old, I heard from a reliable source that Penelope Doncaster, our neighbour on Gloucester Gardens, thought that my dimples made me look like a hug-bunny. That's the nearest parallel I can think of, at present."

"It's really you who ought to have it." Molly furrowed her brow judicially. "Few others could properly appreciate it."

"I'm duty-bound to agree."

"I think I can arrange it." Molly turned from the scenery and looked me in the eye. "If you can do something for me."

"If it is within my power and famously fluid moral guard rails."

"That's what I thought you'd say." Molly moved closer but returned to her practice of addressing the wider countryside. "I just need to be able to rely on your jury vote."

"The best whisky will win, Mrs MacAlistair. If that's Kilcladdich, then I assure you it'll have my vote."

"I need to be able to rely on you, Mister Boisjoly, to vote for Kildrummy."

CHAPTER TWELVE

The Poignant Pertinence of the Pinewood Parable

We were unable to further explore Molly's surprising yet surprisingly familiar proposal, because in that instant Isabette stepped onto the Kildrummy side of the road, where the churchyard forms the out-of-bounds boundary (stroke plus distance) of the sixteenth fairway. Her locks of igneous rocks swirled about her head like a faithful flame, and she was hitching up her skirt for speed.

As she passed, we made our hellos and goodbyes and, as I wanted to take her mind on some important developments, I joined her on the journey to the Kilcladdich side.

"What was all that about?" asked Isabette, setting a panting pace in spite of a basket of rubble on her hip.

"Oh, you know, cabbages and kings." I piffled. "And she wanted to congratulate me on my upcoming martyrdom."

"You mean marriage."

"What did I say?"

"That would explain the pantomime wink she flapped at you."

"She's a velveteen romantic, is our Molly."

"What did you tell her?" Isabette asked, with that deliberate airiness of one making a point of not caring.

"We discussed my trousseau, mainly. She's full of ideas. Can I carry your box of rocks?"

"It's not rocks." Isabette handed over the basket, which turned out to be much heavier than it looked, and it looked like it weighed marginally less than an anchor. "It's baking for the pub."

"Some of your mother's oeuvre?" I gave the basket a little shake, just to hear the clatter.

"It's me that does the baking." Isabette said this with a tone that could have been prideful or vengeful.

"And who could blame you?" I said. "You had a difficult childhood."

"What are you going to do about Mama?" asked Isabette. "She still thinks we're getting married, you know."

"Yes, I've been giving that considerable thought. I don't suppose you and Ludio could just elope, could you? It would cut through a great deal of diplomatic red tape."

"Of course not." Isabette stopped her speed-stalking to face me with her hands on her hips. "What would we live on?"

"Love?"

Isabette resumed walking. "Can you not be an ass, Anty?"

I was going to answer when it occurred to me that the question may have been meant rhetorically, as that particular question so often seems to be, and so I pushed the conversation along more productive lines.

"I'm sorry about your Uncle Duncan."

"Did you do it?"

"I did not."

"Then why are you sorry?"

"We were jolly good mates, Duncan and me." I alleged. "Incidentally, what would you say your views would be of someone who could be described as a 'pan-loafy'? I mean to say, assuming it was a fair assessment."

"You have a very London way of expressing condolences," observed Isabette.

"It's how we cope with loss," I explained. "Do you recall where you were when the distillery exploded?"

"Which one?"

"The latest," I specified. "The one which removed Uncle Duncan from my list of admirers."

"I was talking to Hamish."

"Detective Sergeant Hamish Budge?" I clarified. "I might have known. First thing he asked me was if I did it. Then what did you do?"

"We went to Kildrummy, obviously, fast as we could."

"I must have just missed you."

"You were inside, I think." Isabette stopped, now, as we'd reached the door of the Mash and Mashie. "I carried on to tell my ma what happened."

"Was she at home?"

"Of course."

"See anyone along the way?"

"Just Molly MacAlistair. She was on the bridge. Still is, in fact."

Isabette nodded towards the bridge, which caused me to glance in the same direction, and we both saw Shelby Sheercliffe, steaming into port with a quiver of clubs on her shoulder.

"Did you see Mrs Sheercliffe in your travels?" I asked.

"No," Isabette said, with a whisper of wonder in her voice.

"What ho, tipplers." I announced myself with my subdued, opera box voice, in keeping with the respectful quiet of the Mash and Mashie. Tannin was at the fire, gazing reflectively into a glass of golden agoes. Vickers stood at the bar with a half-pint of some suitably sombre stout. Even Angus and Alistair were only half-heartedly disagreeing about the direction in which tankards should be hung above the bar.

I put my basket of fresh-baked gravel on the bartop, as instructed by Isabette, who entered negotiations with the proprietors.

"When you're at your leisure, Vickers, I'll be upstairs mourning these shoes."

"Have we been hopping on one foot across barnyards in our good Balmorals again, sir?" Vickers held the wreckage up to the grey light of my bedroom window while I addressed the sock question.

"That was a one-time occasion, Vickers, and the result of a dare," I reminded him. "No, this comes from kicking a dory free from a moss island. You'll note the telltale matgrass embedded in the laces and what I suspect is a tadpole in the toe."

I assumed a convalescent position on the bed with a short one that Vickers had brought along while he examined the array of mysterious riches that was our boot box.

"I fear that our footwear options are limited," he announced. "I appear to have reflexively instituted your father's practice when coming to Glen Glennegie of packing the boot box sparingly."

"Presumably in aid of filling it with contraband for the return journey, that it might be introduced into the house under Mama's rigid import restrictions."

"Precisely, sir." Vickers held up the survivors. "Until I've had an opportunity to clean the Balmorals, these two-tone Oxfords, with plain leather sole, are the only alternative."

"They'll suit nicely, Vickers," I claimed. "I've given up off-piste hiking for the duration, and in any case I've divested myself of my ovine detail — don't ask how, the memory is too fresh. Furthermore, choice isn't always what it's cracked up to be, by those who crack up such things."

"Very true, sir."

"I'm referring to our list of suspects, of course."

"I had surmised as much."

"It was a good deal easier when we had only the one murder," I reminisced. "You remember those days, Vickers? It's like it was yesterday. The obvious beneficiaries of the death of Lummy MacAlistair were all neatly organised on the Kildrummy side of the river."

"Most convenient, sir." Vickers spoke distractedly as he constructed a makeshift cobbler's bench on the window sill.

"It certainly was," I agreed. "It seemed obvious that the motive was to end the feud in Kildrummy's favour, with a murder that left Kilcladdich without a master distiller. Now neither distillery has one. This also means, incidentally, that there's no one to set the rules for the next jury, which could easily mean an end to this absurd system, if not an end to both distilleries."

"Could this not still be the motive?" asked Vickers. "I believe you mentioned that Mister Budge had already advanced the theory that there was more than one killer."

"True enough. In any case, clearly something's going on with Yvaine and Molly — they've each tried to buy my vote, for starters."

"Sir?" Vickers straightened from his task and glowered at the very idea.

"It gets worse," I said. "No, actually, it says about the same, qualitatively, but it gets stranger. They're each trying to get me to vote for the competition."

"Mrs MacAlistair wants you to vote for Kildrummy?"

"And Mrs MacAngus wants me to vote for Kilcladdich," I completed. "Odd, what?"

"Most peculiar."

"I wonder if this isn't representative of the whole business," I pondered. "Maybe they're trying to get their family out of the whisky business while there's still something out of which to get."

"Is that probable, sir? Whisky has always been a staple, I would have thought."

"Well, not everywhere is our drawing room," I pointed out. "And according to Tannin, the entire industry's on the slide. She's focussed on the continent these days, and mainly importing French wines rather than exporting Scottish dreams. Says it's mainly down to Prohibition in America."

"A most unfathomable state of affairs."

"Isn't it?" I concurred. "Puts me in mind of Spruce Pinewood, chap I know from the club. He tried prohibition."

"Is prohibition something that individuals can try?"

"It's not," I confirmed. "At least not with any lasting success, and such was the case with Spruce, but he was quite committed to the project at the outset, and for all the usual reasons."

"*Cherchez la femme,*" offered Vickers.

"*Cherchez la* love of his life," I said. "And at first sight, too, it's important to add, because he spotted her one rainy day in Soho. Lost all affection for the bachelor life right there on Portland Place, and followed her into All Souls Langham."

"He followed her to church?"

"He followed her into a church, to be pointedly pedantic, because she was attending a meeting in the cellar."

"I see."

"Not quite, you don't — it was a meeting of the temperance league," I reported. "Spruce had cornered the girl and introduced himself and just short of proposed marriage before he even noticed that the evening's entertainment was a raised platform of irate, middle-aged women in raincoats banging drums and denouncing the evils of a happy life."

"Ah."

"Yes, now you see," I said. "A member of the Juniper, in love with a teetotaller. And this was a chap among chaps who knew how to squeeze the most out of a bottle — he invented the Swingleton, you know; two parts champagne, three parts freestyle saxophone."

"A gentleman of robust appetites," said Vickers to my right Balmoral walking boot, which he wore on his hand like a sockpuppet.

"Very, but, in love he was, and to be fair to Spruce, he stayed the course. Sold off his cellar, cancelled his share of the Juniper's surprise weekly crate of Bacchus-berry juice, and ceded me his standing reservation at Club 43."

"Have you a standing reservation at Club 43?"

"I do not. Turns out the ice sculpture horse on the dance floor was for display purposes only," I reminisced. "But, while I had it, I had a most intriguing encounter there — I met Loulou Tattingswick."

"Very intriguing indeed, sir."

"Loulou was the teetotaller with whom Spruce was in love, Vickers."

"Ah. Thank you for the clarification."

"Pleasure. So Loulou, it turns out, is a secret and yet positively champion soak. Put away a bottle of Bollingers while I was reminding her who I was. Between turns with the house orchestra doing a spirited if not altogether indistinguishable impersonation of Mistinguett, she tells me the whole, back-page truth — she admires Spruce's strength of will and wishes that she could be more like him, but his dedication to the monastic lifestyle has driven her in exactly the other direction. The dry nights in and the improving books and early mornings were just to the other side of what a young London girl could stick, and now would I excuse her, she's spotted a table that badly needs dancing on."

"A most vexing dilemma," opined Vickers.

"Well, no, Vickers, I think you may have missed an important detail," I commented.

"This is likely, sir, I'm somewhat preoccupied by what appear to be teeth marks in the sole of your left boot. What was it that I missed?"

"That which was not there, Vickers — Loulou had not sworn me to secrecy. A little judicious blabbing on my part and the very next day Spruce and I were laughing to distraction about the whole affair over a couple of tall risky and sodas."

"A most satisfactory conclusion."

"Not quite, actually," I said. "Spruce couldn't just spring it on Loulou that he knew her secret, so he conceived a dubious surprise — at tea the following day, he spiked the lemon squash."

"Was that wise, sir?"

"Most manifestly not," I replied. "You see, Loulou decided, independently, to break down Spruce's defences in exactly the same manner and she, too, spiked the lemon squash. All that would have been fine, of course — a considerable improvement on lemon squash, if you ask me — but Spruce had forgotten that his mother and Bishop Seabert-Stroud were invited to tea that day."

"Oh, dear."

"Not a complete disaster," I said. "Spruce told me he'd always wondered what they wore under those cassocks."

"I trust, sir…"

"Secrets, Vickers," I anticipated, and followed up with a short inventory; "Isabette and Ludio's romance. Whatever that poison pen is all about. Shelby Sheercliffe's real reason for being in Glen Glennegie. The mysterious, mythical distillation technique. Indeed, even you and I are harbouring a dark secret."

"Speaking of which, I should mention that I very nearly misspoke, earlier, when fetching your restorative."

"Do they suspect?" Aghast, I very nearly sat up. "I don't need to tell you, Vickers, that what would become of the slightest word would harrow up thy soul, freeze thy young blood, and whatnot."

"You may count on my discretion, sir."

"Discretion." I rationed a sip of whisky to reflection. "This is what strikes me as peculiar about all these secrets."

"Surely by their very nature…"

"I mean there's more to them than just being secrets," I elaborated. "Take Glen Glennegie's very own Romeo and Juliet, Ludio and Isabette. Why don't they just elope? Think how much more smoothly would have turned the wheels of love had Romeo and Juliet just popped off to Messina over much ado about nothing, or gone to Milan with the two gentlemen of Verona."

"Or even to Venice," suggested Vickers, distractedly, as he popped a pebble out of the tread of my boot with what appeared to be a purpose-built whatsit.

"Please, Vickers, you know how I am when Iago comes up in conversation. Perisher. Wish I'd been there."

"I beg your pardon, sir, I had forgotten," retracted Vickers. "Perhaps Miss MacAngus and Mister MacAlistair are unable to quit Glen Glennegie for pecuniary reasons. After all, *il faut manger.*"

"You're right there at the gate with your French aphorisms today, aren't you, Vickers," I observed. "And, yes, one must eat, and in fact that's what Isabette said. And it looks as though Ludio's future as a master distiller has been foreshortened, so have they set aside Romeo and Juliet in favour of a bit of Macbeth?"

"There is as you say, a rich abundance of choice," sympathised Vickers, as he gazed quizzically at something trapped in the boot brush. "Perhaps an examination of the circumstances would reduce the gallery of suspects."

"When has that ever worked for us, Vickers?" I asked. "Certainly in the case of the first explosion we have one of our seemingly impossible murders — there was no one near the distillery when it blew up, and so far as I could tell that was true of the second explosion as well, unless I did it."

"I have every faith in your innocence, sir."

"Thank you, Vickers, I draw strength from your confidence in me. That just leaves Shelby Sheercliffe, according to all available evidence and the prejudices of Detective Sergeant Budge for which, if we're being wholly honest, I'm mostly to blame."

"And yet, if I understand correctly, she remains the only suspect without a motive."

"Unfortunately for her, Vickers, that's no longer the case," I said. "I've worked out her secret."

"Want to know my secret?" said Shelby to Tannin as I joined them at the low table by the fireplace with three small eight-year-old Kildrummy '11s. "Thanks, Boisjoly."

"Which secret is that?" I fitted the frame into a high-backed spectator's seat.

"Whole course theory." Shelby announced this as though she expected it to be met with a lot of scandalised humming and hawing from the house. "Some golfers see each hole, each stroke, as a game in itself or worse, a distraction from a pleasant walk in the country."

"But not you," urged Tannin.

"Whole course theory, which is my own innovation, takes everything — the tee grounds, the greens, fairways, bunkers, bounds, wind and weather — as a single monolithic challenge to be beaten, dominated, crushed under foot."

"I see," I said, lying.

"Then you break it all down, into its constituent parts, so that every stroke becomes part of an overall strategy."

"Isn't that, just, sort of, golf?" I asked.

"Golf is just a game," corrected Shelby. "Whole course theory is a practitioner's guide to life."

"And this doesn't drain any of the fun out of the sport?" I wondered.

"If golf were meant to be fun, Boisjoly, it would be."

Having known a few golfers, particularly some of the walnut-skinned tragedians who rank among the Juniper's most cantankerous under-tippers, I saw her point. These blokes were morose and miffed at the best of times, but when they came in on the weekends, as often as not with a bag of broken clubs and a notarised determination to quit the game in favour of killing themselves with drink, it was with the far-off stare and trembling hand of one who'd been through the wars.

"How was today's good walk spoilt, Mrs Sheercliffe?" I asked.

"Under par."

"I'm sorry to hear that."

"That's a good thing, Anty," pointed out Tannin.

"I'm happy to hear that."

"And then that Budge bloke came along," lamented Shelby. "Stood with his foot right over the eighteenth hole until I answered his carousel of questions twice for every turn — where was I when the second distillery exploded, what about the first distillery, what was I doing when Lummy was blown up, did I recall where I was when the Kildrummy distillery blew up, am I quite sure that I was in the sand bunker on the twelfth fairway when I heard the second explosion, remind him where I was when I heard the first — and so on like that for a good half hour. Is he dim?"

"He's thorough," I explained. "The objective is to keep asking you the same question until you give a different answer, then they can legally hang you."

"I don't know what cause he thinks he has to suspect me."

"Well, you're from London, aren't you," I pointed out. "Or are you?"

"Of course I am."

"Then there you are. From the perspective of our Mister Budge that's a literal confession," I said. "And the detective sergeant believes that you were the only suspect with the opportunity to commit the first murder and, while I doubt it, it's always possible that he's worked out that you had motive."

"What motive?" scoffed Shelby, with the same deliberately dismissive tone with which I fancy Nelson, his telescope to his blind eye, asked, 'What signals?'

"One of the oldest," I explained. "Lummy MacAlistair broke your heart, thirty years ago, when you called yourself Fiona MacAngus."

CHAPTER THIRTEEN

A Go-Getter's Guide to a Greater Game of Golf

I'd seen a number of portrayals of this role, but Shelby's interpretation was standout — strong and self-possessed, she made the part very much her own, swirling her whisky and affecting disinterest in the big reveal. The fire crackled. Tannin cast me a meaningful glance. I smiled vacantly and waited.

Finally she swallowed her drink in a single throw and said, "Not a crime, is it?"

"Murder?"

"Changing your name."

"I think it depends. I expect it's much like doing the shimmy or animal impressions — the legality of which is highly contextual."

"When are animal impressions ever illegal?" asked Shelby.

"In my experience, when in court," I replied. "But it can very much depend on the judge's mood."

"How'd you work it out?"

"The rule books," I said. "You claimed to have read them, which I'm sure you did, but your knowledge of a player's options *'should an honest strike be distrayed by beast, imbecile, or feeble-minded child'* is thirty years out of date."

"That's it? I might have just misremembered."

"Misremembered what?" I asked. "I've examined the rule books and judging by the decades of dust I'm the first to have done so for decades. I still wasn't entirely sure, of course, until just now when you referred to the first deceased as Lummy."

"I knew it as soon as I said it."

"The initial clue, though, was your alleged reason for being here," I added. "To play a course you'd only heard about, to give something back to a town you'd never seen, ostensibly, and that even your late husband only ever visited once every ten years? It raised my suspicions, and put me on the alert for dusty rule books or some variation thereof."

"But, Anty," interjected Tannin. "If Mrs Sheercliffe is from Kildrummy, why hasn't anyone recognised her?"

"Because it's been thirty years," answered Shelby. "I was a slip of a thing, then. Lummy would have recognised me, of course, and Duncan, but they were locked in their distilleries before I got here. Yvaine and Molly aren't from here — I'd never seen either of them until just this week."

"How old were you?" asked Tannin.

Shelby's lower lip folded in on itself. "Seventeen. So was Lummy. He used to write me the worst poetry." She gazed with glistening eyes into the fire, and something she saw there gave her one of those flat, fatalistic smiles.

"Do you want to talk about it?" Tannin gently encouraged.

"Not much to say, really." Shelby shrugged the corners of her mouth. "Love-dove, love-above, love-of, love-shove... How many words rhyme with love, anyway?"

"I don't know," I said. "But I'll bet Ludovic does. In any case, I think Tannin was referring to the engagement and breaking off thereof. You didn't read his poems out in church, did you?"

"No, I most certainly did not," said Shelby meaningfully. "I hardly needed to. No, he used to read them to me in our special, secret spot, just upriver from the bridge, on the Kilcladdich side. A meagre anabranch — so small that it didn't even have a name — broke off from the main artery and where it rejoined there was a little waterfall. It was hidden in a bankside wood and the cascade formed a curtain over a tiny cave. You could walk past it for years, looking right at it, and never notice it."

"A most valuable discovery," I observed. "I know from experience how difficult it is in these two towns for a young romantic to find the privacy a chap needs to pitch his case to management."

"That's certainly true," agreed Shelby. "It was probably more true, then. It was our refuge, our sanctuary. We'd meet behind the waterfall, he'd read me his stupid, sweet poems, and I'd make us a picnic. And I decorated the cave with silly little placeholders — a picture of the Eiffel Tower, with kerchief curtains, that would one day be the window of our flat on the Champs Elysée, a stub of a candle just like the one we'd have on our tiny table under that window, flowers and magazines and books and bits and ridiculous, hopeless hopefuls. We were just playing house, of course."

"Did Lummy not take the long view?" I asked.

"Oh, he was committed," contended Shelby. "I had all the poetry to prove it — he asked me to marry him a hundred times in a hundred clumsy rhymes."

"It's a wonder you let him weasel out of it," ventured Tannin. "A lot of girls would have taken those poems as a legal proposal, and sued for breach of promise."

"I was broken-hearted." Shelby looked wistfully through her whisky at the fire. "And in any case, I had little choice. At first, though, that's how the MacAlistairs saw it — they offered me money to release him. I said no. I was in love."

Shelby smiled at this recollection, the way a chap will do when recounting how he lost his shirt on a nineteen-to-one longshot because he had a good feeling about the horse's name.

"So, then my family offered Lummy some undisclosed amount..." Shelby steadied her voice, which had begun to sound in need of a bit of sanding, with a taste of courage. "...and he took it."

"But you still had the poems," pointed out Tannin. "You could have stitched up quite a substantial suit, I'd have thought."

"They thought of that." Shelby nodded a jealous tribute to her tormentors. "I didn't read Lummy's poetry out in church, but he near as did himself — and he put it about that I wrote them to myself, and signed his name, and that I wanted to be married so badly that I fantasised the whole romance."

"Yesh," said Tannin, neatly capturing the moment.

"To prove the point, he told everyone about our private spot, and showed them my stupid, stupid playhouse."

I still felt it my duty to get to the bottom of the deaths of Lummy MacAlistair and Duncan MacAngus, and I was going to bring the killer to justice, no matter who it turned out to be, but in that moment by that fire with those whiskies and that resigned, wounded woman, I fancied how satisfying it would be to murder Lummy myself.

"The next day," continued Shelby, as if it could get worse, "even the waterfall was gone. Lummy and his father dug an irrigation trench to divert my little stream to the Kilcladdich malt house."

"There was nothing you could do?" pleaded Tannin.

Shelby shook her head with grim conviction. "Not a thing. We'd kept it entirely between us, you see, because of the feud."

"And so you left town," I surmised.

"Wouldn't you?"

"I'd probably leave the country," said Tannin.

"That's just what I did do." Shelby had by now fully recovered her self-possessed, slightly-but-now-wholly-forgiveable bitter stoicism. "Packed everything I had which was, in terms of value, one full train-load of seething cynicism. Took that to London where I turned it into a deep and sturdy trap, and snared Stan Shelby."

"The boot polish tycoon?" I asked.

"None other."

"Shoes that fine should have a Shelby Shine," I recited. "Vickers has a particular affection for 'Obsidian Obsession'."

"It's a big seller." Shelby nodded corporately.

"That might be mostly me," I said. "I ordered Vickers a case for his birthday. That's highly confidential, if it needs be said."

"Doubtless you know that Stan Shelby died from a fatal misjudgement at Lord Messing's hunting lodge," assumed Shelby.

"He was shot?" started Tannin.

"No. He ate an entire pheasant in a single sitting," explained Shelby. "Stan was a man who loved life and living it, to the exclusion of all else, including coronary health. At least he died with a smile on his greasy, greasy lips."

"What a poetic end."

"After Stan, I married Marlon Rushmere."

"The famous sportsman and keen aviator," I recalled.

"Keen, yes," confirmed Shelby. "Talented, no. After that was Emmet Ash-Wickersmith, who believed strongly that when you fall off a horse you need to get right back on. Put that in practice three times in one day, he did. Same horse, too. There wasn't a fourth time."

"You've had some extraordinary luck with husbands," observed Tannin.

"It wasn't all luck," acknowledged Shelby. "You have to know who's going to which parties, and then you need to know how to winnow out an invitation. There's an art to it."

"I mean with regards to them all dying," clarified Tannin.

"Oh, that," said Shelby. "Yes, that was all pure luck. Finally, there was Mortimer. You know, he used to drink Glen Glennegie, and it was among his top two or three favourite topics of conversation, after the recipe for ruin that was the income tax, but I only learned that he was a juror when his invitation arrived in the post."

"He never mentioned it?" I queried.

"I guess he didn't think I'd be interested," speculated Shelby. "Or, more probably, he thought that I would be, and who wants a wife along on a whisky binge?"

"Which brings us neatly back to what brought you here," I summarised.

"Revenge, of course."

"A who now?"

"Revenge." Having fully recovered her form, Shelby swallowed the remains of her whisky in a single throw. "I didn't say anything. I just replied as Shelby Sheercliffe, accepting the invitation in my husband's place. I was going to play it all perfectly straight, too, and just wait to see the look on Lummy's face when he realised who held the deciding vote on the Glen Glennegie jury."

"I'm sorry you missed that," I sympathised.

"So am I." Shelby nodded sad regret.

"You weren't making any efforts to rig the jury, by any chance, were you?" I asked.

"No. Why?"

"What made you think you'd be the deciding vote?"

"It's a figure of speech," said Shelby. "I was always going to vote for whatever you two thought was the winner."

"The voting is anonymous."

"Is it?"

"It is."

"I'll flip a coin, then."

The proposal caught Tannin squarely in both temples, which she massaged firmly.

"You didn't tell all this to Mister Budge, did you?" I asked.

"Are you asking me if I told the detective sergeant that I had a honking great motive for the first murder?"

"I suppose I am, rather, yes."

"No, I didn't, and I'd appreciate if you didn't, either."

"I regret, Shelby…"

"Oh, do come along, Anty," scolded Tannin. "You know that Budge already thinks she did it — he'd stop investigating altogether if he knew about this."

"Nevertheless…"

"At least don't tell him yet." Tannin leaned over the table and lowered her voice. "We're a partnership, after all, right? We should vote on it."

"I vote no," said Shelby.

"It's just Anty and me." Tannin couched hard words in a conciliatory tone. "But I vote no, too, Anty. Just while we investigate."

"Very well," I capitulated. "What did you tell him then?"

"Well, nothing, obviously, about Lummy, and he didn't ask," said Shelby. "He seems mainly concerned with where I was during the second explosion."

"Not the first?" I asked.

"Only because he's sure that he knows where I was, then."

"Yes, of course," I realised. "And where were you during the second explosion?"

"About as far from the Kildrummy distillery as you can be and still be in Kildrummy," claimed Shelby. "I was in the sand bunker on the twelfth fairway. It's a full-on sinkhole, that is, and even if I wasn't up to my pockets in quicksand, the twelfth fairway is a brisk twenty minutes from the road, twenty-five from the river, and even that's when the tide is out."

"Pity you didn't know about the rule regarding signal flares," I said. "Introduced in 1904."

"I didn't know it was a rule, no, but everyone knows about Robert MacAngus and his flaming two-hundred-and-twenty-yard drive."

"You carry a flare gun, then."

"Of course."

"May I see it?"

Shelby unbuttoned a pocket on her canvas and leather golf bin, poked around a bit, and withdrew a handsome brass pistol that looked like it fired something the calibre of a dinner roll. She rifled about a bit more, putting other assorted bits and bitsiers on the table, including a scorebook, a golf ball, a miniature rake that would have made a capital back-scratcher, and a flask.

"No flares." Shelby was peering into the bag.

"How many would you normally expect to find?"

"Two. I always carry two."

"And they're gone, I take it," I took it.

"So it seems."

"Does the detective sergeant know this?" I asked.

"I didn't even know it." Shelby looked up from her search. "He didn't ask about that, either."

"I doubt he knows about the convention," I said. "He says that he's not a golfer."

"He's not," confirmed Shelby. "He asked me why I don't use a bigger ball."

"No!"

"He did."

"The very idea," I mocked. "I say, Shelby, just in case I'm ever asked the same or a similarly nonsensical question, what did you say?"

"I told him the truth," said Shelby plainly. "I said that if he was resorting to asinine questions like that then I would assume the interrogation was at an end."

"I doubt he's entirely satisfied," I opined. "Early returns suggest that everyone can account for their activities during the second explosion, with the notable exceptions of you and me. And if neither of us did it, then it's another impossible murder."

"Then it must have been you, Anty," concluded Tannin, "because I saw Shelby in the sand bunker off the twelfth fairway the moment the distillery exploded."

"Intriguing," I said. "Nevertheless, I still feel quite sure that I didn't do it. You're certain of the time?"

"Very." Tannin nodded resolutely and furrowed her brow authoritatively. "Big, big boom. Giant cloud of smoke. I don't know if you saw me, Shelby, but when I saw you, you very nearly jumped out of your boots."

"So did you," noted Shelby.

"Comes from being a backwoods Londoner, doesn't it?" said Tannin. "I can't even remember the last time a distillery blew up in Marylebone."

"So that's both of you alibied as well," I said. "Maybe I did do it."

Shelby made her excuses with a mannered "Right, then, I'm off," and made merry muddy footprints up the stairs.

"I'm not sure if we've gone forwards or backwards," recapped Tannin neatly. "Shelby's clear of the second murder, at least, but now she has a motive — rather a smashing one, too, giving the female perspective which, I think, is very much within my purview — for the first."

"Speaking of which, did Molly mention anything that could be described as slightly bribey with respect to your vote?"

"She approached you too, did she?"

"She did," I confirmed. "Offered me a hundred-and-fifty-year-old case of Glen Glennegie for my often-imitated, never-duplicated virtue, but here's the peculiar bit…"

"She wants you to vote for Kildrummy."

"Just so," I said. "You too?"

"Offered me the same case." Tannin nodded with a slyly sarcastic squint. "At least, I assume it's the same case. Shall we split it?"

"Did Yvaine make a similar proposal?"

Tannin added a dash of cynical inevitability to her sardonic squint. "Offered me exclusive distribution of all Glen Glennegie production."

"They must know we'd never compromise our vote."

"Do they?" wondered Tannin. "Yvaine didn't even know that I already have exclusive distribution of all Glen Glennegie production. The women were never really involved in the jury before, remember, and, for that matter, neither were we."

"I might add, now you have me thinking of my reputation as an adorable scamp, that the last time either of them saw me I was cutting a romantically roguish figure in the prisoner's dock."

"There you go."

"That goes some distance to explaining why they think they can throw the match," I said. "Doesn't aid much in determining why they'd want to."

"You think they'd kill their master distillers to work it?"

"Tallying what we know so far, I'd have to say that's a solid concrete perhaps," I concluded. "But there's still Ludio and Isabette, assuming they're operating as a team, who might easily have wanted to accelerate their inheritances."

"What inheritances?"

"I just assumed that there are inheritances. Are there not?"

"Not as such, no," explained Tannin. "The way my father explained it to me, the distilleries belong to the towns, and the distilleries are the only things of any worth on either side of the river. Furthermore, Isabette is Duncan's niece, not his next of kin, and Ludio is Lummy's nephew."

"Is simple control of the distilleries worth anything?"

"Honestly, Anty, not a lot." Tannin shifted her chair closer to mine and took up her glass, in the manner of a theatre prop. "If you tell anyone this you didn't hear it from me — you and the Juniper aren't enough to keep two distilleries in operation. You'll remember what I was saying about Prohibition in America... well, that, and changing tastes and this whole 'end of an era' business with the stock market crash, taken together — or, really, pick any one — it means there's really not much time or hope left to save Glen Glennegie."

"Things have taken a serious turn," I concluded.

"More serious than murder?"

"Let us say, with broader repercussions," I amended. "I can attest personally that any disruption to the supply of Glen Glennegie would be keenly felt on both sides of the house and in several key areas of Buckingham Palace. I suppose that's inevitable now, though."

"Is it?" asked Tannin. "Why for?"

"Isn't it?" I asked right back. "I would have thought that among the core requirements, along with quality malt, pure, Scottish river water, and educated oak barrels, you'd need a distillery and a distiller, both of each of which has been assiduously dismantled."

"There's not that much to a still, really, Anty." Tannin shrugged, somehow, reflectively. "There's a big kettle and pipes and valves and pots and any number of doohickies, depending on the type of still. They can be repaired by a competent plumber."

"It would have to be a very competent plumber indeed to put Duncan and Lummy together again."

"No, that's true," agreed Tannin. "Distilling requires a bit of technical skill and something that I think you and I can agree to just call 'poetry'. I suppose until someone's trained up Angus and Alistair could manage."

"The battling barmen?"

"Why not?"

"Presumably the same reason I'm not a master distiller," I said. "I don't know anything about distilling."

"They do," claimed Tannin. "They were both journeyman distillers in their day, and the laws of physics have changed very little since then."

I surreptitiously surveyed the bar, as one does when giving the impression that one is looking at nothing in particular, and rested my gaze on Angus and Alistair, who in that moment were conducting a spirited enquiry into who was responsible for a mildewed scrubbing-up sponge.

"So, you don't think that the explosions were the work of anyone trying to bring an end to whisky production in Glen Glennegie," I deduced.

"No one is that evil. How could you even think that?"

"If you want to get anywhere in this detecting business, Agent Tanners, you need to be prepared to return the steely stare of man's worst instincts with a firm and forthright 'fie'. However, I take your point. We're still a convincing motive or two short of what my friend and collaborator, Wittersham of the Yard, would call 'a useful contribution'."

"For what amounts to two impossible murders."

"And only one certain motive, about which I'm sworn to secrecy."

"Well…"

"Well?" I echoed.

"I guess, I suppose, it could be argued that Shelby has a motive for the second murder, too."

"Oh?" I studied Tannin with my grown-up face. "And when did this occur to you?"

"I'd say, around about the very moment when you said that Shelby was really Fiona MacAngus, the girl that Molly told me had been engaged to Lummy," recalled Tannin. "She also said that it was Duncan MacAngus who made the arrangements with Lummy. It would have been he who orchestrated the all-inclusive heartbreak and public humiliation."

CHAPTER FOURTEEN

The Deeply Sinking Trap and the Two Quart Handicap

"Ach, ya fishnet umbrella, you're a good lad, but you're as replaceable as a divot, you are."

"Is that so, ya half pound of wit in twelve stone of thick. And where would you be without me to tell you which end of a tassie is up and which bit of a goose is down?"

These frank and fair assessments by and of Angus and Alistair issued from my carefully casual question regarding their chosen career paths, re not distilling. Tannin had ascended to her room, leaving me alone at the bar to speak truth and revelation with the barmen.

"As I understand it, then," I summarised, "you, Angus, elected to join Alistair in running the Mash and Mashie because he would have otherwise 'drowned in a dishpan', and you, Alistair, did the same, to save Angus from 'setting fire to the ice block'."

"If anyone could manage it," Alistair put a proud paternal hand on his colleague's shoulder, "it would be him."

"And neither of you miss the tumult and fury of steaming ethanol out of fermented wort?"

"In the case of Alistair," explained Angus in a sympathetic tone, "who has all the taste and talent of a cup of tepid tea he was, in Duncan's view, far too exacting and assiduous to produce the quality of turpentine demanded by the discerning drinker of Kildrummy's finest fermentation."

"And as for Angus," continued Alistair, in much the same vein, "who approached malting and distilling with the delicacy and discretion a disinterested mason might bring to, say, mixing cement, nevertheless failed to see eye-to-eye with Lummy on the matter of keeping the quality of Kilcladdich on a level consistent with the effluence from the nation's finer paper mills."

"It's all for the good, in any case, Mister Boisjoly." Angus spoke and smiled and simultaneously relit his pipe. "I could hardly leave Alistair here on his own to serve Kildrummy to customers who'd innocently ordered a whisky, and were expecting a whisky."

"And though I could never stop Angus from offering unsuspecting punters a Kilcladdich," added Alistair, as he knocked out his own pipe, "I can at least be on hand to administer first aid."

Our attention was drawn in that moment as the door opened and a broad silhouette was cut from the drizzly outdoors.

"What ho, Budgers?" I called. "Sip of something snug?"

Budge made straight for the fireside where he disgorged himself from his greatcoat and spread both he and it on chairs to dry.

"Don't mind if I do, Boisjoly."

It's in my nature to revel in the happiness of others, but I think most people would agree that there's something fundamentally disturbing about a happy policeman. They're rarely celebrating the innocence of someone wrongly suspected or the rehabilitation of a career criminal or a fine day with nothing to report. Typically, in fact, when a policeman is happy it almost always means that someone else is not. I collected eight-year Kilcladdich and Kildrummy '19s and, after much clanging of bells, proceeded to investigate.

"Cheers for that, Boisjoly." Budge took up his whisky and cradled it neat. He delighted, briefly, in the vapours, tasted it, and pronounced it, "Tap."

"You're looking delighted to be knighted." I took the chair across from him. "Make a major arrest, did you?"

"Not yet." Budge eyed the barmen and lowered his voice. "Not yet, but it's just a matter of one final piece of the puzzle. Have you seen Mrs Sheercliffe, by the way?"

This wasn't my first crossing of the chaotic seas of kept confidence in the good ship Foolhardy Undertaking — indeed, it might be convincingly argued that rashly giving my word to keep a secret is something of an area of special expertise — but I don't ever recall being in this deep before. I decided — very much flipping a mental coin — that the best course was a complete blank. A memory hole. I could hardly slip up and tell Budge about Shelby's motives for murder if I hadn't spoken to her at all.

"No, not recently," I said, adding, "At least, I don't think so," in some feral instinct to cover all eventualities. "Have you?"

Budge smiled serenely, like a beat constable finally taking his boots off at the end of a trying day, and rewarded himself with the rest of his whisky.

"My round, I think." Budge took himself to the bar and when he returned it was with two large ones. He took the seat next to me and leaned toward me. "You'll remember our gentleman's agreement, won't you Mister Boisjoly?"

"Agreement?"

"With respect to attribution of... well, of credit," Budge looked shyly into his glass. "I very much appreciate your assistance, but when it comes time to make an arrest, I trust you'll keep your participation discreet."

Another secret to keep. I was losing track.

"You'll want to be mindful of secrets, DS Budge," I warned. "They have a way of getting out of hand, such as with the case of a clubmate of mine, Spruce Pinewood."

"That's a coincidence."

"You know Spruce Pinewood? I didn't think he'd ever been north of Regents Park."

"No, I mean about his name being Spruce."

"Ah, no, that's a sobriquet," I explained. "Essentially a requirement at the Juniper."

"Oh, I see."

"His real name is Woodrow." I refocused my faculties with a quick tickle of whisky. "But do you mind if we stay with Spruce for the telling? It'll help things tick along more smoothly."

"As you like."

And I recounted the twisty history of Spruce Pinewood and Loulou Tattingswick, starting with the thunderstrike in Soho and leading to the meeting of the temperance busybodies at All Souls Langham and from there to Club 43. I remembered, while there, a number of tangential stories, but it was once again my round. When I returned, I'd forgotten the old stories but remembered some new ones. Once I got to the other side of them, though, I had to pause while Budge got us two of the Kildrummy '14s he'd heard such good things about. In time I got over the finish line.

"So, they both wanted you to tell their secrets," worked out Budge.

"S'more to it than that, Bludge," I said. "What I often leave out of this anecdote, for dramatic effect, is the punchline — you'll recall that Spruce followed Loulou into a temperance meeting."

"I do recall that, yes." Budge focused hard as he said that, and finished his whisky.

"And henceforth Spruce tried the dry life, such that he might win Loulou's hand, and in the process causing two people to harbour a gnawing secret."

"Yes." Budge tried again to finish his whisky, but was only reminded that his glass was empty. He looked sad.

"And this is the punchline — Loulou went into All Souls Langham that day to get out of the rain. She had no idea that there was a temperance meeting, and she assumed that it was Spruce who was teetotal."

Budge stared blankly at me for about the length of a chorus of *Brochan Lom,* and then exploded with a burst of laughter the strength and sincerity of which is beyond the might of most sane men. Slowly the quake eased into decreasing and intermittent chortles, then a hiccough or two, and finally Budge wiped away a tear.

"What were we talking about?"

"Secrets," I reminded him.

"What about 'em?"

"Some secrets are meant to be told," I preached. "S'all they're good for."

Budge nodded sage accord.

"Another round?"

"I say, Budge," I said, "when did you last eat something?"

"How long ago was breakfast?"

"I think a bit too long." I shifted toward the bar. "I'll see what they've got that pairs well with whisky."

Nothing, it turned out, was available until dinner time, when Molly was expected with a delivery of pies. I knew, in my wibbly, wobbly way, that Budge and I had miscalculated, and that we needed to eat something, especially if we were going to have another round. There on the bar, as it happened, was Isabette's basket of hand-baked paving stones. I ordered us another round to help wash them down.

"What's that?" asked Budge.

"Kildrummy '26," I answered. "I thought we should ease up a bit."

"I mean in the basket."

"They're not doing food yet. There's just these scones and shortbreads."

Budge selected a scone and felt its heft. "Solid."

"Isabette baked them," I said. "From an old family recipe that apparently calls for limestone."

"I'll bet they're lovely." Budge slurred to Isabette's defence. "You know something, Boisjoly, that's a bonny lass, that is, and I have cause to believe that I'm in with a chance."

"But she's engaged to me," I pointed out. "And Ludovic, I think."

"I'm asking you, Mister Boisjoly, to stand aside, for her sake," stuttered Budge. "Girl like that wants one of her own kind."

"Steady on, Detective Sergeant."

"You know what I mean — someone with a shared upbringing, a love of the land and language. I'll give you a very fine example, if you like."

"I think that would be extremely helpful," I said, for some reason.

"We've had all this whisky, Mister Jobly, and I'm barely feeling it, but look at you."

"What about me?"

"You're all blurry 'round the edges."

"That's nothing to do with being from London or not being Scots."

"It is though," insisted Budge. "Tell you what — you've never played golf."

"I have not."

"Neither have I, but I'll bet you anything you'd care to that I'm a natural, compared to you, do you know why?"

"Because you're Scots?"

"No… I mean to say, that's right."

And that's how it was that Budge and I both arrived at the otherwise inscrutable conclusion that the best and only course of action was to borrow the antique clubs from the walls of the Mash and Mashie and test our mettle on the golf course.

We found our way to what might as well have been the first tee ground — a mound of gravel just across the road from the pub.

"I'll just start us off," announced Budge. "Hold my coat."

"With pleasure," I said. "Where is it?"

We both carefully examined the immediate area before concluding that Budge must have left his coat in the pub, freeing him to line up his first shot. He selected, I think, a cleek, warmed up with a couple of practice swings, and said, "We'll be wanting a ball, I think."

I didn't have one. Budge didn't have one. Again we searched the area, reasoning that we might find a discarded ball or that it was something that a well-appointed course would provide, like teeing sand.

"I've got you," I announced, realising that I had forgotten to let go of the basket of baking. I handed over a roundish rock bun and Budge teed it up.

As I watched Budge teeter over the tee I saw that there would never be a better moment to take his frank views on the investigation as it stood, and perhaps to subtly guide him toward a more broadminded perspective.

"Why were you asking after Mrs Sheercliffe, earlier, by the way?"

"I neglected to pose to her some very meaningful questions," said Budge, distractedly, "regarding flares."

Budge was one of those quick-draw drivers who, once he's set up his shot and his line, wastes not a second drawing back and pulling the trigger. In a blur, he struck the rock bun a blinder, perhaps a bit high on the crust, for a promising first drive of about three yards.

"You spoke to her, then." I chose a small but aerodynamic shortbread man and stood him on the tee mound.

"She says she was on the links when Duncan MacAngus was blown up." Budge spoke with a 'we both men of the world, we know better' sort of implied wink. "So, that part's clear enough, but I've interviewed her. Searched her room. I can find no connection between her and the victims, but for an odd note."

"You searched her rooms?"

"Just being thorough," said Budge, defensively.

"Did you search my rooms?"

"Didn't need to. At any rate, yours was locked."

"Regarding this odd note," I said. "It wasn't a poison pen, was it?"

"How do you come to know that?"

"It was only my first guess," I explained. "My second was going to be a love letter to Cornelius Vanderbilt."

"Well, you're right," acknowledged Budge. "It was a letter warning someone — it wasn't addressed — not to trust Yvaine MacAngus."

"Is there any hope of analysing the handwriting?"

Budge scowled in study. "No, I don't think that will prove a fruitful line of enquiry. I'd need honest writing samples from all concerned... experts... and in any case... it was typed."

I brought to mind a scattering smattering of golf advice I'd overheard and willfully ignored over the years. I kept my eye on the shortbread man, legs steady, knees slightly bent or very straight — I couldn't recall which, so I did one of each — and swung for a very respectable twelve yards, the little man turning cartwheels all the way.

"Very lucky," lauded Budge, with the generosity of the hopelessly confident. He took up the mashie and lined himself up over this rock cake. "Now, I've spoken to everyone else, and all of them, to a man and woman, have someone to vouch for them at the time. I was with Isabette — cracking girl, that — who followed on to her mother's straight after the explosion, so we know where they were."

Budge's baking had been in long grass, but with a novel technique he dug it out, along with about two pounds of good Scottish clay, and moved the lot of it along the fairway some ten yards.

Perhaps to frame this unprecedented success as commonplace, Budge continued with his narrative. He pointed casually with his club toward the bridge. "I passed Molly and Ludovic MacAlistair up there."

My next shot would have been a personal best had it been allowed to stand, but as it was it struck a stone boundary fence and smashed into a thousand pieces, and knocked a chip out of the fence.

"What of Angus and Alistair?" I mentally docked myself a stroke and selected from the basket a sturdy scone. It was more discus than ball but I was able to give Budge the honour by about half a yard.

"What of Angus and Alistair?" Budge's next shot was a bad slice. The right slice bounced into the water hazard and the left went out of bounds beneath a mailbox next to the pub. "They were together, of course."

Budge and I focused on our short game, a strategy which took us for a while down different paths, only meeting once to trade the mashie for the niblick, or vice-versa, and again when Budge needed to replace his ball, his previous having been swallowed whole by a vole.

We reconvened on the fourth tee ground, having somehow misplaced the second and third holes. By this time I had established a creditable lead of ninety-six to Budge's hundred and three.

"But Mrs Sheercliffe has no one to confirm that she was on the golf course." I fetched my shortbread man, who was now just a shortbread head, a clean clip that sent him into a hedge.

"She says as much herself." Budge hooked his toffee square so badly that it landed behind us.

"Are you quite certain that no one saw her, Budgits?" I asked. "I recall with great clarity your words regarding rote police work — stirring stuff, if you don't mind my saying so — neither inkling nor intuition, just the committed, careful cataloguing of questions and claims by a hard-working rozzer. I'm convinced, Budgins, that if you keep at it you'll find someone who can back up Mrs Sheercliffe's version of events."

"What makes you think that?"

"Hunch?"

Budge tallied five more strokes, none of which moved his toffee, but did result in some fairly extensive landscaping that cleared a clean eyeline to the fairway, and on the sixth try he hit a long fade to the dogleg, where it landed in a stand of casual water and dissolved.

"You know where you could be of use, Bojilly, is in the matter of motive. It's something of which the Advocates Depute can be quite particular."

This, obviously, put me very much at odds with myself — I had a duty to report what I knew, and I had given my word not to. I opted for strategic procrastination and went looking for my ball.

One hedge looks very much like the next, after six or seven whiskies, and even moreso after however many it was I'd had, and I resigned my shortbread head to nostalgia, took a stroke and distance and an oatcake.

We met next at the seventh green, which is on the edge of the gorge about equidistant between the road and the water, and at the centre of a broad mudflat. By now my lead had stretched to a nearly unassailable one hundred and sixty-six to two hundred and one. The confidence I gleaned from this unanticipated talent for the game caught me up at this point, though, when I chipped my oatcake in a casual arc towards the green only for it to come down two yards short, with a splat, and sink three inches into the mud.

Budge, who was now playing with a clootie dumpling, popped it very neatly to within a yard of the pin, and we both stood at the edge of the slurry sea and considered our options.

"You'll note," I said, gesturing across the wide, barren plain, "that anyone taking an interest in firing a flare into that distillery from behind, and then appearing on the seventh green by the time the fire brigade arrived, would have to cross Satan's Surprise Party," I gestured with my niblick towards the aptly named bunker formed of deep marshes, organically disguised as a picnic lawn, "the expanse of the sixth fairway," which was not only half a mile wide but positively hollow with rabbit warrens, "and the length of this moore of mire."

"Aye, that's true." Budge followed my niblick, nodding knowingly. "I wonder how she did it."

"She couldn't have. This is my point."

"Must have done." Budge began delicately following a stepstone path to the green, arms spread like a tightrope walker.

"Not unless she could fly, she couldn't. And how do you suppose she ever made such an extraordinary shot with a flare gun?"

Budge wavered on a stepstone and looked at the distillery, which was now becoming something of a silhouette in the growing gloom of evening.

"She must have been hiding on the ground floor." Budge stroked his chin and nodded approval of the motion.

"She'd have been blown to bits herself."

Budge hopped dismissively onto the green. "The explosion was contained to the upper floor — that's why it was so... ehm, explosive."

"Then how did she shoot a flare through a solid wooden floor?" I asked.

"She cut a hole, first."

"Did you find such a hole?"

"No." Budge crouched behind his dumpling and shut one eye, the better to line up the last twenty-two inches to the hole. "But there was one in the floor of the Kildrummy distillery. Just about flare-sized, now I think of it."

"But we know that Duncan cut that himself," I reminded him. "Did you find an axe, as indicated?"

"I did." Budge paused here to meticulously miss the hole by a foot. "It was blown clear by the explosion, but I found it stuck in the door. You were very lucky it missed you."

"I have lightning reflexes," I explained and then, almost as if to prove the point, slipped and sat in the mud and, tangentially, remembered that I had promised Vickers that I wouldn't take my two-tone Oxfords into the wild.

Budge potted his coolie dumpling in an exacting six putts and I took four to determine that my oatcake wouldn't fit in the hole. Budge conceded the stroke like a gentleman, and the score stood at one hundred and seventy-two to two hundred and nine.

The sun was setting and a heavy mist was rolling in off the sea and the eighth hole was fully the other side of Kilcladdich from where we stood, at the top of an incline so steep and rocky that a rope ladder had been installed for the benefit of beginners and the infirm. We elected to switch out for rock buns, which had proven themselves by far the most resilient and spherical of

Isabette's repertoire, and drive from the seventh green to the ninth fairway.

Budge teed up his bun on a generous mound of mud. "I expect you think you're ahead."

"Only in the mathematical sense," I encouraged.

"Well, that's all about to change, Mister Belljelly — you see, I'm not left-handed."

"I didn't think you were."

"You won't have noticed, then, that I've been playing left-handed until now."

"No you haven't."

"Aye, I have." Budge gripped his mashie with a sly smile, which then broke. "Oh. No, I haven't."

"Do you think we ought?" I offered. "I frankly doubt it would make a great deal of difference."

Targeting the ninth hole from the seventh green has the advantage of circumventing a tricky depression on the one side of the ninth fairway and the north sea on the other, effectively narrowing the approach to roughly eleven inches. A knotty drive at the best of times, and there was a bit of a breeze beginning to express itself.

Budge's line was impeccable — thirty yards up and over the fringe, then dropped straight down for a perfect lie. I had less luck, and hooked badly into the river, twice, before settling on a strategy of putting my way to the fairway. By the time I got there, the game was square at two hundred and ten.

"Did you say that you thought you were in with a chance with Isabette?" I asked as we stood at the end of the ninth fairway, side by side, looking at the ninth hole on Moan Innes, surrounded by swirling black currents.

"I did." Budge took a practice swing that accidentally connected and pitched his bun onto the island, a yard from the cup. "Between you and me, Bill Jelly, she told me that she expected to soon be shot of Glen Glennegie and everyone in it. I took that to include Ludovic MacAlistair."

"Curious. Did Ludio express a view on this?"

"I don't think he knows," speculated Budge. "His plans are more local. He means to establish Glen Glennegie's first 'maizon litter air', such as he's heard of sweeping Paris."

"He's right," I confirmed. "If you can't defend a view on the construction of identity in *A la recherche du temps perdu* at *Les Deux Magots* these days, you'd better be prepared to stand at the bar. Why do you suppose it is that Isabette and Ludio elected to confide so much in you?"

"S'like I said." Budge nodded sagely. "We seek the spame language."

Returning to the match, I adopted the same, casual approach that had worked so well for Budge, and overshot the island by about ten yards.

"What you want is a bit of Scottish in your system." Budge produced a handsome pewter flask from his waistcoat. It was true that a penetrating wind was coming from the sea, now, and that current stores of heating fuel were dangerously depleted. We both stocked up to what I can admit in retrospect was an ill-judged degree.

With eighteen strokes I sent as many rock buns — the entire inventory — into the roiling river, before finally landing a shard of buttery next to Budge's bun on Moan Innes.

"We continue by water, Budgins."

"In that?" Budge referred, obviously, to the leaky little skiff.

"I can handle her, Captain," I said. "I rowed at Oxford. I also fell into the river at Oxford. I'm prepared for all contingencies, including, if it comes to it, finessing the sash of the porter's lodge at Waterhouse, should we be out past curfew."

We wobbled aboard and pushed off and I immediately had to call upon the skill and spirit they drill into a chap on the Oxford second-tier rowing squad. The river was higher than it had been earlier in the day, and the playfully robust Kilcladdich side, already more imposing than the calmer currents of Kildrummy, was asserting the fixed view that where our little boat really ought to go was Denmark.

"It's fair to say, Budgers, that you've made your point. It's also fair to say it's raining ice water," I said as I pulled us across the Straits of Kilcladdich. "What do you say we make this the final hole, come what may?"

"Spoken like a gentleman," slurred Budge. "You're not ahead, are you?"

"You are," I reminded him. "By, let's call it, nine."

We agreed terms and squelched onto Moan Innes, sinking to our ankles and schlorping out again as we safaried to the legendary ninth hole.

"It can't be far," I claimed. "We didn't pass any other islands along the way, did we?"

"It's gone," concluded Budge, and I daresay he was right. We were dead centre of the island, precisely where only minutes before we'd seen a smooth, flat green with a hole in it, and where now there was only a surface best described as river.

"I say, Budge, when, roughly, does runoff season begin in the region?" I asked.

"It varies," said Budge, pensively. "But typically it starts around the end of January, and lasts until about the middle of December."

Either the river began to roar at that moment or I just then noticed it, but certainly the water level rose in a sudden, sweeping rush as I recalled that Angus and Alistair had warned that Moan Innes can sink entirely during runoff season.

"Budge," I announced. "I concede the match. Smartly played. Let us toast your talent for golf and my talent for quitting on dry land in dry footwear."

The water was very near our knees, now, but even as we turned back toward the boat we saw it bobbing jauntily in the waves as it floated past us and out into the open sea.

CHAPTER FIFTEEN

No Respectable Intellectual Wears Non-Prescription Spectacles

"Do you know what would be dashed handy right now?" I said to Budge. "A signal flare."

"I was thinking that very thing," replied Budge, as the waters rose around us and he gazed longingly at the shore. "You think we might be able to swim it?"

"It occurs to me that if we're going to try, we ought to head to the Kildrummy side."

We surveyed the field. A hard-working rain was falling straight down in great, solid, sea-worthy fists of cold water, and the river was widening around us. The Kildrummy side was further, but the water was appreciably calmer, notwithstanding ephemeral eddies and whirlpools that seemed to pop in and out of existence with a certain deadly capriciousness. They were, however, to take the positive view, increasingly difficult to see in the dark.

"You stay here, Boisjoly." Budge spoke with the sober authority of a man standing to his knees in freezing water. "I'll get help."

"In fact, Budgums, I was going to propose something along similar lines," I countered. "The drunken river crawl is rather in the way of being a speciality of mine. I'll be somewhat handicapped by the absence of full evening dress, but I expect it's like riding a bicycle."

"Hold on, Boisjoly." Budge held my sleeve like the constable he once was.

"I really think I need to get started."

"Yes, I believe you do." Budge spoke with a worryingly fatalistic calm, like those chappies in some sun-scorched strip of empire, holding the fort against ten thousand indignant indigenous and discovering they're down to one bullet and barely enough tea for a pot. "I'm afraid that my feet are stuck in the mud, old man."

"Put your hand on my shoulder and give a good kick."

"It's no good, Boisjoly. It's like standing in cement." Budge was hit in the back of the head by a particularly seasonal wave. "Listen, should I not make it through, do me this one service in my memory, will you?"

"You have my word as a gentleman, HMS Budge, but you're going to get through this."

"Just be the best possible man you can for Isabette." Budge paused here to allow a portion of felled tree to float between us. "Oh, and, if you wouldn't mind, bring Mrs Sheercliffe to justice, will you? I'll put in a word for you up there."

"If she did it," I promised. "I'll see that she pays for it."

"Thank you. You'd best be off."

"I would do," I said. "But I appear to be stuck as well. You're quite right — I've never stood ankle-deep in cement, but I'll wager it feels exactly like this. Rather... definite, if you will, in a blood-curdling sort of way."

We struggled for a bit, employing one another's shoulders in scientific lever techniques and, if anything, we pushed ourselves deeper into the mossy bed.

"Perhaps the water won't get much higher," I suggested. Indeed, we were up to our hips, now, but that was mainly down to our efforts to free ourselves — the water level had remained constant within reason.

"I feel I'm still sinking." Budge put a hand on the surface of the water, about waistcoat level.

"Yes, I daresay we are."

"If I could just know Mrs Sheercliffe's motive," lamented Budge. "It's bad enough drowning without finishing the job."

"Listen, Budgely, I'm not saying that Shelby Sheercliffe killed anyone." I stopped for a moment to swallow a mouthful of muddy water. "But — and I recognise that you probably feel I ought to have mentioned this sooner — but her real name is Fiona MacAngus and thirty years ago she was engaged to be married to Lummy MacAlistair."

"I… see."

"Oh, and, in for a penny… It was Duncan MacAngus who brokered the severing of the engagement, and the public humiliation of Fiona, aka, Shelby Sheercliffe."

"Mister Boisjoly…"

"The reason I haven't said anything until now, if I may take the liberty of anticipating your point, is that I was under an obligation."

"Very well." Budge regarded the sky with undisguised resentment. "Doubtless all this will be worked out in time by my replacement. Probably that over-educated Sergeant MacTavish — he wears spectacles for show. What kind of a policeman wears spectacles for show?"

"I have an idea," I said. "And, as it's mine, you need to let me execute it, no arguments. I'm going to go underwater and pull your feet out of the mud. Then you must swim to the Kildrummy side, using all your strength, including that with which you're doubtless planning to refuse."

"It's a good idea, Boisjoly, and it's certainly our best hope, but it has to be me who goes under."

"Sorry." I held up the hand of staunch refusal. "It was my idea. My idea, my privilege. Are you ready?"

"No, Boisjoly — it has to be you who goes ashore. I can't swim."

"Can't swim?"

"I never learned."

"You really should have, Budgers. I know you think it's the sort of thing you'll never need, but, well, now look at you."

"I expect this is goodbye, Boisjoly. All set?"

"Wait! Budgers!"

"It's no good, Boisjoly. No sense both of us drowning. That would leave Isabette with Ludovic, and between you and me, he's a bit of a pan-loafy."

"No, I mean, look there, on the bank."

On the Kilcladdich side, precisely where I'd abandoned them, my flock of loyal followers had gathered at the river's edge.

"Coyly," I called to the big-eyed lamb, who had struck me as the most ready-witted of a largely incurious community, "go for help."

Coyly didn't go for help. He just stared anxiously at us from the bank and danced nervously from hoof to hoof. This approach to the problem was soon picked up by the others, and presently the river bank was a crowd of ineffectually wobbling wool.

"Right," I said to Budge. "Where were we?"

"Would you fancy that?"

I followed Budge's baffled gaze back to the sheep who were, extraordinarily, wobbling into the water. The biggest and beefiest prop forwards, three or four abreast, marched directly into the rushing currents which swirled indifferently around them. I realised, finally, that the Kilcladdich side of the river was so fast and frenetic because it was shallow — shallow enough to be forded by the sort of steel-willed sheep they grow in the north of Scotland.

The wall of wool positioned itself at what would be the edges of the island, if it had still been there, and with a slow and splashy collapse, I fell within reach. I steadied myself on a veteran, grandfatherly sort, and towed Budge free of the grip of Moan Innes. Hand over horn, we pulled ourselves along the sheep causeway to the safety of the shore.

☙

"Is that tea, Vickers?" I called out, in bare and brittle tones, from beneath the morning blanket.

"It is, sir." Vickers clattered and clanged what sounded like a tray of church bells and loose change onto the side table.

"It smells of sea-sick." I pulled the blankets over my head. "Everything smells of sea-sick. Take this morning away, Vickers, and bring me a better one."

"I regret, sir…"

"No, I know." I emerged from the covers just enough to face my responsibilities. "My own fault. And that of Detective Sergeant Budge, to no small degree. Scottish blood, indeed. Some things, Vickers, are inherited, like an intolerance for golf."

"Doubtless so."

"While others, such as an appreciation and capacity for whisky, are acquired through astonishingly irresponsible parenting." I reached for my cup of steeped sunrise. "Oosh, Vickers — there's a storm approaching. I can feel it in my joints. And my temples."

"In fact, sir, the weather is already quite inclement."

I looked to the window and learned that the rush and hiss that I'd assumed was internal was the voice of a North Sea gale, complete with heavy precipitation.

"Doesn't mean there's not *another* storm coming," I contended. "Anyway, I feel *something* in my joints. Feels like ice water and despair. What do you suppose that means, Vickers? I could be coming down with something."

"I think not, sir."

"No, once again, no one else to blame," I acknowledged. "In fact, Budge turns out to be made of quality artisanal ingredients. He tried to sacrifice himself for me on the river."

"Indeed, sir?"

"Claimed he couldn't swim, when only seconds prior he was insisting that he be the one to go for help," I recounted. "He's still the perfect habitat in which to rear and raise a healthy prejudice, but I find myself thinking he's not, to employ a distilling metaphor, all heart and no head."

At this point the gale slapped a sheet of seawater against the window. I huggled myself into my burrow of bed.

"I shall take breakfast right here, Vickers, if and when I ever regain my appetite. That goes for all my meals, until further notice or next Christmas dinner, whichever comes first."

"I fear, sir, that you'll have to rise eventually today," advised Vickers, who was already menacing me with my last clean set of tweeds.

"Am I being knighted today, Vickers?" I asked. "Am I scheduled to address the House of Lords? No? No, I'm not, and there's nothing so pressing that it can't be put off until I've completed my convalescence or simply passed away peacefully."

"Today is the day of the Glen Glennegie jury."

"Already?" I marvelled. "Have you noticed something rummy, Vickers, about playing nine drunken holes of golf with baked goods and then nearly drowning in a freezing river during runoff season? It causes time to elapse in a most unusual fashion. One is aware of the hours passing, but it feels rather as though they ought not count. How long do I have?"

"It's approaching noon, now, and if your whisky palate is to be in mid-season form by this evening, you'll need time to repair and prepare your constitution."

"What do you suggest?"

"As much sweet tea as you feel you can manage," prescribed Vickers. "Then a lengthy bath, followed by more tea and two slices of toast and marmalade. Above all, you must not exert yourself until you feel you can stomach a substantial breakfast."

"It's an exacting regime, Vickers, but people are counting on me."

"Precisely, sir."

"Nevertheless, it rather nobbles us with respect to the ongoing investigation."

"I assumed that by now you had resolved both puzzles."

"And I have," I said. "Just about, in any case, but there remains a final test that needs doing, and it involves rather a lot of running about in heavy weather."

"I would be most glad to undertake the task on your behalf," said Vickers, as he topped up my cup and set about stirring it into a syrup. "If you'll furnish me with precise instructions, I'll be on my way."

"I assumed as much, Vickers, and your *esprit de corps* is noted, but this requires younger legs. I need you to take a message — a most confidential message — to my partner in crime-solving."

"Very good, sir."

"Once we've all gathered downstairs for the tasting, Tannin must find a suitable moment to slip out — doubtless I'll be able to orchestrate some distraction and, in fact, I think I feel one coming on now — then, moving from just above the sand bunker on the twelfth fairway, where Mrs Sheercliffe said she was during the second explosion, to the Kilcladdich distillery, and timing her movements precisely — and this is the important part, Vickers — she must plot a course that would have been undetected after the explosion."

ẽ

"Ach, ya sad symptom, you're as quick off the mark as the mark."

"Am I now, ya open-toed welly. Well, I'll certainly take that comment to heart, should I ever hear it from someone who isn't all bag and no pipe."

This brisk market of opinion was already posting gains when I wobbled on failing legs to the bar, where I steadied myself and waited for an opening in which to make a bid on a palate cleanser. In the meantime, I took a short census.

Budge was alone by the door, listing in an armchair and nursing his head and a tall glass of water that looked, in my state, sublime. Isabette and Yvaine occupied a table on the other side of the door from him and they appeared to be discussing something in low tones, such that their flowing crimson coifs combined like the Red Sea reunited. Similarly, Molly, in purple evening curtain, and Ludovic, in a copper-coloured waistcoat, huddled over a couple of small ones on the upholstered bench beneath a window, looking like Rosencrantz and Gildenstern waiting on the dock for Hamlet. Shelby was fully occupying one of the high-backed chairs by the fireplace, swirling a large one and glaring dark thoughts at Budge. Across from her, Tannin sat alert and sly, crinkling a conspiratorial corner of her eye at me.

The fire crackled and hissed and waved wobbly, warm yellows about the room, meeting and matching the storm that whistled and drummed at the windows.

"Are sheep all right in this weather?" I asked the barmen.

"Are the sheep all right in this weather?" echoed Angus. "Of course they are, Mister Boisjoly, because they're not out in it."

"They're usually indoors long before most drunken idiots have to be rescued from Moan Innes," added Alistair, "but last night was a special treat for them. Since then they've been put where it's dry."

"Yes, quite." I adjusted my tie contritely. "I hope that you'll extend my gratitude to the keeper of the flock."

"Happy to be of service." Angus lit a casual calabash.

"It is Angus you'll want to thank," deferred Alistair. "Seeing as it was he that neglected to close the barn last night."

"That's true," confessed Angus. "I'm often remiss in checking that Alistair has done his turn at the finishing up."

"Just a tick," I said. "Do you mean to say that those are your sheep?"

"Half of them are mine." Alistair puffed life into his clay pipe.

"And half are mine," calculated Angus.

"But when I asked whose sheep they were you said you didn't know."

"No," Alistair stickled, "we said that they might be Jock Mackie's lot, which they weren't."

"And we asked if any of them were wearing hats," quibbled Angus. "Which they also weren't."

"We never said they weren't our sheep," summed up Alistair.

"No, fair enough," I fibbed. "As a matter of pure curiosity, though, why did you let them follow me all over the course?"

"They like you." Angus said this with thinly disguised surprise.

"And you have a talent for grazing sheep." Alistair, too, spoke with wonder in his voice.

"Took them all over the glen..." observed Angus.

"And I hardly have time to do all that," concluded Alistair, "and all the while keep an eye on Angus."

"No, I can see how that would be trying, what with keeping a lid on this hotbed of commerce and running the Glen Glennegie jury every ten years." I tapped the heavy glass cabinet of contestant whisky. "Talking of which, isn't it just about time for the bathing suit round?"

"The cabinet stays locked until six o'clock." Angus nodded at the clock, which showed a full ten minutes before the starting pistol. "Then Alistair takes charge of the Kildrummy swill." Angus waved dismissively at the upper shelf of the cabinet, with ten bottles, each hand-labelled for the distillery and year. "I manage the Kilcladdich, of course."

"There are ten bottles for each distillery," continued Angus. "One bottle for every year, starting from 1915, aged for however long the master distiller decides."

"So the longest possible age is fourteen years," calculated Alistair, "and the shortest is three."

"The master distiller will select the barrel the day it's put down, and monitor it for years," recounted Angus. "In the case of Kilcladdich, Lummy chose a range, and tested them year-on-year. The Kildrummy choice was made, I expect, by throwing a dart in the dark."

"What an auspicious occasion." I moved casually to the end of the bar. "I think I ought to say a few words in honour of absent friends and Glen Glennegies past." I glanced at Tannin and with subtle but sophisticated eyebrow semaphore, drew her attention to the bell. She rose and wandered across the room as one just stretching her legs. There was a moment of perfect calm but for the storm, and even it seemed to hush and swoosh in suspense.

"Hear ye, hear ye…" I called and, simultaneously, I seized the key and rang the bell like my ship was sinking.

The penetrating peal of a bell — particularly a stout, brass, schoolmistress bell like this one — is very much what all loud noises sound like on a heavy and head-achey morning after. It's what being struck on the bridge of the nose with an oar would sound like if it were audible and enduring. It sings, it stings, it rings with eye-shutting oppression.

It's probably impossible to measure the protective value of putting tightly shut eyes between a ringing bell and a heroic hangover, but that's what I did. Nevertheless, I was aware of the population of the pub closing in around me and urging me to rethink my current course of action.

I held the line for as long as possible, only finally relenting to Budge's beseeching, "Mister Boisjoly, please, for the love of all that's good in this world, stop."

I stopped. I could still hear a singular pitch in my skull, but that would pass with the years.

"What ho, Budgers." When I opened my eyes it was, I discovered, a group exercise. Budge afore me and the bar abaft, Molly and Ludio to port and Yvaine and Isabette starboard, and all of us emerging from a collective, strained squint.

"Did you have some cause, Mister Boisjoly, to ring the bell?" asked Alistair.

"The usage of which is quite clearly reserved for the orderly operation of the bar," added Angus.

"Oh, you know, just felt inspired, as one does. Propitious moment, and all that, the inauguration of this decade's Glen Glennegie jury. Thought the occasion wanted for a few weighty words."

"Well, then?" Molly crossed her arms in a way that also said 'Well, then?'

"Me? Oh, right oh. Well, unaccustomed as I am, and all that… what ho, Glen Glennegie!"

Response was muted. In fact response was staring silence, because as I finished my speech I gestured toward the cabinet of candidates, in the manner of introducing the guest of honour, as it were, and everyone of course looked. What they saw, though, brought a startling end to proceedings — the cabinet was still locked, the bottles were still there, but the labels were gone.

"How is that possible?" Budge approached the cabinet like an ornithologist approaching a pterodactyl. He tested the door and determined that it was, indeed, locked. He examined the shelves and the area around the cabinet.

"It doesn't matter *how* it was done," contended Yvaine. "Why would anyone do such a thing? This disqualifies both candidates — it's the end of Glen Glennegie."

"It doesn't matter how or why," was Molly's take on things. "Find out who did it, and we'll soon enough know the rest."

The spirit of the mob continued in this vein for a bit until I brought order by simply raising my hand.

"If you ring that bell again, Mister Boisjoly," said Alistair with dark implication, "you're barred for life."

"I thought you might like to know how it was done," I explained. "Not to mention why and by whom."

"You mean to say that you know how it was that someone, while you were holding the key in your hand, opened a locked cabinet, removed all the labels, and locked the cabinet again?" doubted Angus.

"Oh, right, yes, that too," I said. "But I've also worked out how, by whom, and why the murders were committed."

CHAPTER SIXTEEN

Of Secrets and Timing and Dubious Rhyming

The squall skirled and it surrounded the pub, rattling the door and brattling the window. All attention turned to me but for that of Budge, who was struggling to put on his greatcoat.

"Your explanations will not be required, Mister Boisjoly," he announced with a certain enervated, final-mile commitment to the cause. "I'm ready to make an arrest."

"I know you are, Budgings, but if you'll hear me out you'll be more ready yet, complete with means, motive, and method."

"I already have all that." Budge glowered what he probably thought was a prosecutorial leer at Shelby, but the effect was undermined by his continuing and clearly hopeless battle with his greatcoat.

"Then if you'll agree terms with your coat and stay awhile, you'll also get that elusive fourth corner of an airtight case that no advocate depute has ever been able to resist — a confession."

The psychology of the career-minded rozzer with an historic hangover is roughly as complex and involved as the inner workings of a ceramic thimble and, accordingly, Budge ceased struggling with his greatcoat and collapsed into a high-backed chair.

"All right, then."

Drawing on the allure of the man with the secret, I composed my court about me by the fire and called upon my enchanters and mead.

"Perhaps a large one all round, landlords. The wind blows cold outside and I'm in a state best viewed through glassware."

"Age, year, and label?" asked Angus.

"Only one way to tell, I think." I gazed longingly at the candidate cabinet. "Is it so that both distilleries are officially disqualified?"

"It is," pronounced Angus and Alistair simultaneously.

"Right, then, let's start with any one of those, and I'll ask you to keep careful note, respectively, as I perform my forensic analysis."

Angus and Alistair considered this unprecedented proposal with a frank and detailed exchange of pipe smoke and scowls. Finally, Angus unhooked the key from the bell, approached the cabinet, and failed to open it.

"It's the wrong key."

"Of course it's the wrong key," I said. "All such illusions always turn out to be disappointingly simple — someone was able to unlock and lock the cabinet while the key hung from the bell because the key hanging from the bell is a room key. All that was required was a distraction, first provided by my sheep, and then provided by me."

"But, where's the real key?" asked Alistair.

"Well, you could determine that by process of elimination," I proposed. "That key, obviously, fits the door of the room of the person who has the real key."

Angus started for the stairs but I spoke up again, "Or, Mrs Sheercliffe, you could just admit that you have the key. It would save a bit of time and I confess to a strong medical need for half a draught of hair of the dog."

Shelby, who had been sitting across from Budge and anticipating this moment, gave me one of those weary, 'you-think-you're-so-clever' looks that I collect by the dozen. She produced the key from her pocket.

"I admit, Mister Boisjoly, I didn't think you were actually going to deliver a confession." Budge struggled with the idea of standing and, presumably, effecting an arrest.

"There are many more confessions to follow," I assured him. "But they'll come easier and quicker with a little tonic from the tree of truth. If you please, Angus?"

Angus retrieved the key from Shelby and opened the cabinet. He and Alistair removed the bottles and arranged an amber glass forest on the tables between us, twinkling in the firelight.

"An '18, certainly," I adjudged a sip from the first random sample. "One can easily taste the heavy rains and consequent early barley harvest... I'm going to say Kildrummy — I detect Duncan's famously light hand with the river water."

This was met with general agreement, including and especially from Budge, who held his glass and gazed out at the storm and warmed to the idea of tales by the fireside.

"Let's have it, then, Boisjoly — what else have you got to reveal?"

"Secrets, Budgington," I said. "The theme and theory of everything that's happened here in Glen Glennegie over the last few days, and indeed, over the last thirty years."

"No reason to go into all that, Boisjoly." Shelby spoke idly, though, and examined the flames through her whisky.

"I'm not referring to only your secrets, Mrs Sheercliffe. We have a full catalogue of confidences to get through, in fact, starting with those of Spruce Pinewood."

"We've heard this one," complained Ludovic.

"It is a corker, though," countered Budge.

"It's true," I agreed, "it is a corker, but it's not true that you've heard it all. There's one final detail that I left out of the story of two young lovers keeping the same secret from one another. Loulou wanted Spruce to know that she wasn't teetotal, and so when she met me at Club 43, she deliberately failed to swear me to secrecy. The twist in this tale is that Spruce had already worked out that Loulou was a connoisseur of the blurry early hours, and he ceded me his standing reservation at the club in the strong and specific hope that what would happen is exactly what did happen."

I poured us each a sampler from the next bottle, dwelt for a moment in its bouquet, and tasted it.

"Kilcladdich '23," I declared. "And, if I'm not mistaken, the distilleries will have exchanged several barrels that year."

"Correct," said Angus.

"How is that of any relevance to us?" asked Molly.

"Barrel rotation, Mrs MacAlistiar, is of concern to all right-thinking people."

"I mean your Spruce Pinewood story."

"Ah, of course," I realised. "Some secrets, you see, are meant to be told, isn't that right, Isabette?"

"I don't know what you mean," said Isabette with that sing-songy insouciance of one who knows exactly what I mean.

"There's nothing more credible than a revealed confidence," I continued. "If I were to tell you, Budgits, that I think your moustache gives you the gravitas of a retired general, you'd dismiss it for hollow flattery. But if Vickers were to tell you that I'd told him in strictest confidence that your moustache filled me with an emerald green envy, you'd take it dearly to heart, would you not?"

"Oh, well, thank you, Mister Boisjoly." Budge combed down his moustache with both hands.

"Well, we're dealing in the main with hypotheticals here, but you're welcome," I said. "At any rate, this is the psychology behind the complex conspiracy of Ludio and Isabette — they wanted me to reveal that they were in love, and intended to marry."

"Anty!" scolded Isabette.

"Isabette!" scolded Yvaine.

"They wanted me to reveal it, Mrs MacAngus, but it was never true," I said. "Few things are in this region, but what *is* true is that there aren't a lot of ways to turn a profit outside of the whisky trade, and that the MacAngus and MacAlistair families share a lasting animosity."

"Confirmed," said Shelby.

"And so how does an intelligent young lady finance four years at Edinburgh University? The reverse dowry." I paused here to select my next sample and allow Yvaine time to try to set fire to Ludovic with a hard stare.

"What is a reverse dowry?" asked Budge, thankfully.

"One of the great traditions of the family feud," I explained. "Typically, it's a payment made to a young lady so that she might release from his commitments the favoured son of a society family with a solid reputation for hypocrisy which they work tirelessly to maintain."

"But in this case you mean Lummy MacAlistair," reasoned Budge.

"No, I don't," I differed. "The story of Lummy and Fiona is well known in the community, and it's the inspiration for Isabette's plan — she and Ludio aren't engaged — they're spectacularly ill-suited to each other — but they wanted their families to hear that they were and offer one or the other a settlement to end it. Then, they'd split the money and pursue their dreams. They swore me to secrecy and assumed I'd break my word because of my fame for repeating the story of Molly and the vicar, and when Isabette learned that it was in fact Budge who had betrayed that particular confidence, they placed their contrived confidence in him."

"Oh, well, thanks very much, Anty." Isabette didn't actually sound very grateful at all.

"You wanted your secret told," I pointed out. "I told it. I tried to warn you off with the instructive parable of Coals Stokely."

"Of course." Ludovic snapped his fingers. "I say, that's really very clever, Anty."

"Your mistake — I mean, apart from embarking on this mad plan in the first place — was swearing me to secrecy," I preached to Isabette. "Even when you contrived to have your mother catch us alone in my room, I remained a man of my word."

"Your own kin." Molly spoke to Ludovic with an aggrieved, Shakespearean wail.

"A fair condemnation, Mrs MacAlistair," I acknowledged, "but one that would carry a good deal more weight coming from someone who wasn't herself secretly planning to betray her family."

"I never…"

"Stood a chance?" I completed for her. "You're right, you didn't. It's astonishing the degree to which so much of what has occurred has hinged on my poor reputation. Isabette thought I could be relied on to betray her trust, you thought I could be bribed, and Yvaine thought the same."

I allowed that notion to steep while I analysed the next specimen, "Kilcladdich '15, obviously. I recall the '14 well — my father and I shared a bottle to mark the occasion of my mother's departure for a tour of the Americas — and this picks up precisely where that left off in terms of trace notions of charcoal, walnut, and kelp."

"Why would my mother want to bribe you?" asked Isabette.

"Like Mrs MacAlistair, she was trying to throw the jury."

"But, why?" asked Ludovic.

"They were being paid to," I explained. "By Mrs Sheercliffe, who came to Glen Glennegie to kill that which she hated most in the world..."

Budge raised his eyebrows at this and considered it carefully, eventually settling on an official reaction of "Oh-HO!"

"She came to Glen Glennegie to kill the feud," I clarified for the record. "The single source of her life's defining heartbreak."

"What heartbreak?" Molly asked this in the tone of one about to elaborate on the theme with some variation of 'Let *me* tell *you* about heartbreak.'

"I'm Fiona MacAngus," said Shelby.

"Oh," acquiesced Molly, and then appeared to look for something at the bottom of her glass.

"Just two ticks, if you will," Yvaine interjected into the sombre moment. "You were paying us both to nobble our distillery?"

"She was," I confirmed. "Or, put another way, she wasn't paying either of you. To understand Mrs Sheercliffe's approach one must become a student of 'Whole Course Theory' — she wasn't trying to sway the jury, she was trying to corrupt it. Why pay to accomplish that which can be done for nothing, with a holistic understanding of the straight-line-simplicity of the psychology of feuding families?"

"What psychology?" asked Molly, as one who had heard of the concept, but regarded it with homey suspicion.

"The feuding family psychology," I rephrased. "You agreed to try to get your entry disqualified, correct? By failing to deliver your candidate bottles or by trying to bribe the officials, and the arrangement was that you'd be paid if you subsequently lost."

Molly and Yvaine spoke some slant on "That's right," with slow surmise.

"And what would happen if you were both disqualified?" I asked. "Neither of you would be paid, and the Glen Glennegie label would be awarded to neither distillery."

"Am I to understand that you ladies are only just now learning that you each had competing arrangements?" asked Budge. "If that's so, then who wrote the poison pens to Mrs Sheercliffe, or who was she writing them to?"

"She wrote them, Budgems, to herself," I reported. "Put more accurately, she wrote them for you and me — when she thought that I was the town gossip, she slipped a letter into Vickers' pocket, assuming that I would spread the word. When that failed and, like Isabette, she'd learned that you, Budgestetter, were the real public information service, she left one in plain view in her room knowing, or at the very least hoping, that you'd search it, in light of your oft-stated presuppositions."

"To what end?" Budge directed this to Shelby, who replied with the quiet confidence of the veteran boxer with a lucky horseshoe in his glove.

"To enliven competition, I expect," I mainly speculated. "I assume that Mrs MacAngus and Mrs MacAlistair initially tried to interfere with the entries, but that would have given Lummy and Duncan the time needed to provide new ones, which is why Mrs Sheercliffe herself delivered the Kildrummy entry, and slipped it into the cabinet while we were distracted by the traditional running of the sheep."

"But, why would you agree to such a thing, Mama?" demanded Isabette.

"I know it's always been your dream to go to university, or at least live near one," answered Yvaine. "You were never very clear on which."

"Oh. I didn't know. I'm sorry I tried to trick you into paying me to end my fake engagement."

"Perfectly understandable temptations," I decreed. "As already shrewdly observed, there aren't a lot of avenues for turning a profit here in Glen Glennegie, and even the whisky business is getting tighter — Mrs MacAngus and Mrs MacAlistair had only two things worth selling — the Glen Glennegie jury and the course rules."

"You worked that out too, did you Boisjoly?"

"Oh, yes," I said. "I've known for certain since… oh, since just this very second… that you had pitted Mrs MacAngus and Mrs MacAlistair against each other in a bidding war to merge the course rules. The only way that the poison pen letters make sense is if you were trying to drive down a price, but since you never intended to pay for nullifying the jury, it must have been something else — something of value, something both women could influence as the senior tee ladies, and something that would contribute to ending the feud."

"Merging the course rules was harmless and, if we're being honest, long overdue," said Yvaine.

"But disqualifying both distilleries," continued Molly, "that's brought an end to Glen Glennegie, forever."

"Hardly," I said. "This is yet another secret that was no secret at all — the end of the jury system was never going to be the end of Glen Glennegie, just the absurd division of resources that prevented the brand from realising its full potential. The point was to force the families to negotiate a new set of rules, something that had always been an option…"

"But not while Lummy and Duncan lived," realised Yvaine.

This was followed by a period of reflective pause, during which the storm splattered and battered the pub in a four-walled assault on our well-stocked fortress. I interviewed the next applicant.

"Kildrummy '20 or '21," I quickly concluded. "Green and piney and pure… smells of fresh rains and a new decade."

Budge refilled his glass from the Kildrummy '20 or '21 and gazed over it at the window, which in that moment was slapped with some seaweed and a mackerel. He sighed deeply, doubtless in anticipation of the final reveal.

"So, we know why she did it," he summarised, drawing a curtain on the evening's entertainments.

"Well, we still haven't worked out how, yet, Budgeling," I pointed out. "And I promised you a confession."

"I have worked out how she did it, in fact, Mister Boisjoly," reported Budge.

"I don't think you have," I doubted.

Budge nodded sadly. "You remember the story of Robert MacAngus?"

"You're not going to suggest that Mrs Sheercliffe drove a burning flare over six hundred yards and potted it through a six-inch vent, are you?" I asked. "Twice."

"Is that unlikely?"

"It's impossible," said Shelby.

"Well, with all due respect, madame," said Budge, "you would say that, wouldn't you?"

"Not if I'd done it," differed Shelby. "I'd be taking out ads in *The Times.*"

"Then how was it done?" despaired Budge.

"I thought you wanted a confession," I recalled.

"Can't I have both?"

"There's nothing I can refuse that cherubic dial, Budgeman," I said. "You may. The method by which two men appear to have been murdered in locked distilleries with no one around is, inevitably, simple, and I can explain it now, if you like."

"I would like that, yes."

"For the confession, however, you'll have to wait until my junior partner has tested a theory."

"Say, where is Miss Tibbits?" asked Budge.

"Testing a theory," I said. "I should have mentioned that."

"Why? What theory?"

"I sent her to Kildrummy because I require her absence," I announced, "while I tell you how she murdered Duncan MacAngus."

CHAPTER SEVENTEEN

A Meditation on Aeration, Predication and Causation

"But you just said that Shelby Sheercliffe did the murders." Budge put his whisky down with the halting reluctance of a policeman remembering that he's a policeman. He stood and walked to the window, presumably looking for Tannin, but he was met with a wall of pressed rain and the howl of a sou'easter with a strong personality.

"I didn't, actually, Budgerly," I said. "If you'll refer to the fourth reel, you'll find that I established that it was Mrs Sheercliffe who did the cabinet trick, nobbled both sides in the whisky challenge, and sparked a bidding war for control of the much-prized Glen Glennegie golf club rules. I can see how one might lose track in that Genesis five of misdemeanours, but I feel quite sure that never did I say that she'd killed anyone. I'm not saying definitively that she didn't, you understand, merely that she hasn't killed anyone here and lately."

"Well, it was certainly never Miss Tibbits either," contended Budge. "She wasn't even here for the first murder."

"Nobody was, Budgement — there was no first murder. Lummy MacAlistair blew himself up by accident and Tannin Tibbits seized the opportunity to stage two seemingly impossible murders, at least one for which she could not possibly be a suspect."

"An accident?"

"You'll recall, DS Budge, that we were both struck by the extraordinary timing of events — most notably two consecutive explosions and two men independently discovering the same secret at the same time. This fully impossible coincidence becomes a good deal less coincidental if it was all predicated on a single event — an accident."

"So, the whisky did get him, after all." Molly nodded knowingly.

"In the sense that it led as it so often does to careless smoking," I amended.

"Lummy didn't smoke," corrected Molly.

"He smoked like a malt house on fire, Mrs MacAlistair, just never around you. He also restricted his gambling, cursing, and telling the one about you and the vicar to moments when he knew that he was unobserved, which I expect was at least part of the impetus for locking himself into his distillery."

"But what about the flare we found?" asked Isabette. "How did that get there?"

"Tannin put it there," I explained. "When I left the Mash and Mashie to investigate and Mrs Sheercliffe returned from golfing, Tannin had her inspiration — she would make an accident look like murder. She went to Mrs Sheercliffe's room — which of course wasn't locked, since the key was already hanging from that bell — and borrowed the flare gun that she remembered would be there from packing her father's golf bag, including a dozen spare niblicks. While there, she must have scattered several golf balls about the room, but time was of the essence — she hurried to her own room and shot a flare into the rain barrel which is directly beneath her window, resulting in the sooty rainwater which Angus blamed on Alistair and, obviously, Alistair blamed on Angus. Then she went to the distillery — ostensibly to tell me about the arrival of Mrs Sheercliffe — and discreetly dropped the spent flare under cover of smoke and ash."

"That cunning jackal." Shelby pronounced this with a finely-tuned balance of praise and pique.

"Yes," I said. "She already had her plan, and it already involved you, didn't it?"

"She took me for a perfect ride." Shelby shook her head admiringly.

"You two were conspiring, you thought, to invalidate the jury," I continued. "It was she that provided the candidate bottles of Kildrummy, wasn't it?"

"It was."

"Which she acquired," I explained, "when she told Duncan the secret process."

"So, there really is a secret process." Yvaine, I think, said that, but it was a widely murmured sentiment.

"There most definitely is not a secret process," I said. "Or at any rate, not one that works. But Tannin worked out instantly what Lummy thought it was, and she shared it with Duncan so that he would put himself at the same risk by exposing the methanol to the open air and cutting a hole in the floor of his distillery with an axe, causing the room to fill with smoke. This is why Angus and Alistair couldn't agree on whether or not Duncan was burning off the head or the heart — there wasn't enough smoke from the chimney, but the air smelled strongly of methanol."

"He's lucky he didn't choke to death," observed Yvaine, with no discernable trace of irony.

"I expect he nearly did," I said. "I think that Tannin took the precaution of putting a wedge in the door, and Duncan was trying to break it down when the explosion occurred. It would account for the axe that Detective Sergeant Budge found stuck in the door."

"None of that explains how she — or anyone — managed to shoot a flare into the distillery," claimed Yvaine.

"That is explained by another disappointingly simple illusion — she was on the ground floor, by the furnace, and she fired the flare through the hole that Duncan helpfully provided."

"She'd have been blown to bits."

"No," said Budge, nodding realisation. "She wouldn't have been. Both explosions were contained — it's why they did so much damage inside but very little without. But I thought she was here at the time."

"She was on the Kildrummy side, shooting a flare through the floor," I corrected. "She returned by boat, under cover of fog, which is why the boat was on the Kilcladdich side when I needed it to slip my entourage. And that, in fact, was her fatal error."

"Taking the boat?" suggested Ludovic, presumably just to have made a contribution.

"Accidentally claiming to be in two places at once," I said. "She gave Mrs Sheercliffe a false alibi — you didn't really see her on the course, did you, Mrs Sheercliffe?"

"No," admitted Shelby. "I thought she was just helping me out, so I said I saw her, too."

"She was helping herself, twice," I said. "She gave herself an alibi for the time of the explosion, and she kept you in the clear because she still needed you to nobble the jury. However, less than twenty minutes later she was here, on this side of the river, even though Mrs MacAlistair had been on the bridge the entire afternoon, and saw no one cross but myself, Isabette, Detective Sergeant Budge, and Angus and Alistair, in that order and to that extent."

"Crossing a river by boat doesn't prove anything," pointed out Yvaine.

"Not on its own, no," I conceded. "But doing so clandestinely is quite suggestive, and Tannin was here when I returned from the distillery. Later, she claimed to have seen Mrs Sheercliffe in the sand bunker on the twelfth fairway when the distillery blew up. She didn't know — although she does now, I expect — that this is fully twenty-five minutes from the river."

"It's a sound theory," judged Budge.

"Thank you. It's also the only possible explanation. If she'd been where she said she was, Mrs Sheercliffe would have seen her and the boat would still have been on the Kilcladdich side, where Mrs MacAlistair and Ludovic saw it only minutes before. No one but Tannin Tibbits could have killed Duncan MacAlistair."

"But she's also the only one without any cause to do so."

"On the contrary, DS Budging, she had the strongest reason of any of us — stacks and stacks of money."

"How does killing Duncan MacAngus accomplish that?" puzzled Budge.

"Without the death of Lummy MacAlistair, it doesn't," I acknowledged. "Taken as part of a larger, explosion-based strategy, it achieves what Mrs Sheercliffe set out to do but wouldn't have — it ends the jury system. Corrupting this one contest would never have finished it — as Mrs MacAngus explained to me, the stubborn pride of the master distillers, handed down over the generations, would have simply re-established it or something very like it. But with both men gone and no one to replace them, the distilleries would have had no choice but to join forces and, consequently, massively increase production of a supply for which Tannin has exclusive distribution rights."

"But she told us that the market was drying up," pointed out Budge.

"Yes, she did, didn't she?" I recalled. "I'll remind you that she also killed a man — I'm going to suggest that she's not a reliable source."

"But, America's made drink illegal..." Budge's comment trailed away in wonder and awe.

"And you yourself pointed out that it was unsustainable," I reminded him. "You were right, it is. In fact, Prohibition has already failed, as I know from fond and foggy memories of New York's upper west side, and as we heard from Tannin herself."

"I knew it."

"I know you knew it, Budgers. And so did Tannin, of course, but she wanted us to believe that she did not, which is why, to belabour the theme, she made it sound like another secret, to lend it credibility, when in fact it's only a matter of a short period of time before Prohibition is repealed and she could exploit those American distribution channels her father had established. All she needed was a quality product, and plenty of it."

A wide-eyed silence followed this summation. The wind wailed outside and the firelight flickered. Budge nodded in that very specific, sage way that people do when their presuppositions about Londoners are confirmed.

"Why do you think she'll just confess when she comes back?"

"Comes back, Budgeman?" I queried. "She's not coming back. Tannin has run away."

"Run away? How was she ever going to confess if she's run away?"

"Running away is a confession. You told me you needed a concrete case to present to the Advocate Depute, but Tannin Tibbits is a woman of singular intelligence. She was never going to just confess, so I had Vickers ask her to navigate a discreet path between where she said she'd been during the first explosion and the Kilcladdich side of the river. As soon as she realised how far that was, she knew that she was found out, and doubtless went directly to the train station."

"You let a murderer escape?"

"I arranged for a murderer to escape," I gently corrected. "You're welcome."

Budge stared at the storm. The storm stared back.

"I'll have to get a cable to London."

"Plenty of time for that, and there remain many secrets yet to reveal," I said. "However, if you feel you must be excused early, we can start with yours."

CHAPTER EIGHTEEN

The Startling Series of Successively Stranger Secrets

Budge had surrounded himself almost entirely with greatcoat as I spoke, and his hand was on the door handle. Outside the gale wailed and the rain caned and he looked like a man who would welcome an excuse to dally.

"My secret?" Budge glanced shyly at Isabette. "Oh, right, mine. Very well…"

"Not that one, DS Budge, I refer to your ambition to rise in the ranks, and the one thing that's holding you back."

"Letting killers escape?"

"A top-level education."

"It's no more a man's disgrace to be born poor than it's to his credit to be born rich," Budge pointed out.

"Nevertheless," I pointed right back, "you can correct the oversight, provided I'm right about two critical suppositions."

"Very well…"

"It was you who, ten years ago, during a night of abandon and whist, obtained from Lummy MacAlistair the one about Molly and the vicar, and a case of what is now a hundred-and-fifty-year-old Glen Glennegie."

"I was going to mention it," claimed Budge. "But you kept going on about how much it was worth."

"Bringing us to the second supposition — you haven't drunk it all yet."

"Couldn't bring myself to." Budge again stole a glance at Isabette. "I could never find the right occasion."

"On behalf of the Juniper Gentlemen's Club, future Inspector Budge, I'm prepared to offer fifty pounds a bottle," I said.

"Would five hundred pounds secure you the education you require?"

"Thank you very much, Mister Boisjoly."

"You might want to help him pick out a school, Isabette," I said. "I know it's something of an area of special expertise."

"I can't afford it either," sulked Isabette. "And I don't have any hundred-and-fifty-year-old case of whisky to sell."

"You have something infinitely more valuable," I assured her. "You have a Boisjoly who has finally got over the fact that you read out his poetry in church. Mrs Sheercliffe will establish a Glen Glennegie scholarship, and you'll be its first beneficiary."

"Charity is very much not a part of Whole Course Theory, Boisjoly," reported Shelby. "In fact, there's a whole chapter about never conceding a stroke."

"I don't doubt it, but you'll pay for a scholarship and you'll rebuild the distilleries, providing for increased and increasing production, and in return I'll reveal the most valuable secret of all."

"Go on, then."

"Bluebells."

"What about them?"

I rose on aching pins and hobbled with my restorative — Kildrummy '19, with the inexplicably chocolatey aftertaste and yet nose of mahogany smoke — to the painting of the river.

"The *soi-disant* secret process supposedly dates back to the famous game, held in 1767 because historically it was, obviously, historical. But something else happened that same year, something of far greater consequence — the ninth green was created on Moan Innes."

I pointed with my whisky hand at the painting of the island, bristling and blowing with bluebells.

"And so the island ceased to be a source of peat, the single greatest influence on the personality of a whisky apart from ageing," I explained. "Peat remained plentiful, though, and the division of resources that followed the golf match meant that nobody took note of the change of source, or if anyone did it was buried by time and ancient animosity."

"Bluebells…" said Angus, as though speaking the name of a long lost love.

"Aye…" agreed Alistair.

"I feel confident that a taste of pre-match whisky will bear me out," I said. "I look very much forward to being borne out."

"We'll need a master distiller," observed Yvaine.

"You'll need two master distillers," I incremented. "To keep pace with the increased production. And in any case Angus and Alistair come as a set."

"They hate each other," protested Shelby.

"They don't, in fact," I differed. "On the contrary, they're probably the closest friends this town has ever produced. They operate a pub together and share a herd of sheep. I'll wager they'll both happily return to a trade that the feud forced them to quit, so long as they do it together."

"I can hardly let this poor call for guardrails on a footpath operate complex machinery like valves and doorknobs without supervision, now, can I?" pointed out Alistair.

"I confess I'll need the help," conceded Angus, "and Alistair's a dab hand at licking postage stamps, determining if a liquid is wet, and counting and recalling all the positions of an on/off switch."

"There you go," I said to Shelby. "The Mash and Mashie now only needs management that's less preoccupied with the distinctions between one whisky and the next."

"Oh, I say." Ludovic raised his head and then waved his hand. "I could do it. Honestly, I can't tell one from the other. Can't even really tell whisky from brandy."

"The perfect barman should be void of judgement and brimming with poetry," I decreed, "and above all he should never ring a bell."

There was much enthusiastic toasting of this proposal.

"With the merging and, I assume, enormous simplification of the course rulebook," I continued the distribution of happy endings, "management of both the distillery and golf course can be done by the tee ladies."

"We'll be needing to get on with it straight away," said Molly to Yvaine.

"Starting with a substantial cheque," said Yvaine to Shelby.

"Where's the fire? I don't care to be rushed," said Shelby to no one in particular.

"Neither does whisky," I noted. "It's aged for at least three years, and I wouldn't be even remotely surprised if Prohibition was repealed in America as early as 1933."

The storm voiced support for urgency. The windows were now swirling black with cloud and fog and evening. Into the gloom of the room a light appeared from the stairs, accompanied by the shuffling dignity of an heirloom valet, just waking up from a medically-prescribed afternoon drift.

It's never certain where Vickers will find himself when he awakes. He came to the light one Sunday last March and straight away laid out my grandfather's Royal Rifles parade uniform in anticipation of my attendance at the wedding of Prince George, the social event of 1893. Made for a dashed clumsy Easter cricket match at Richmond Green, particularly as I was first bowler.

I mused on this and the Kilcladdich '20 — sawdusty, but not too sawdusty — and watched in detached horror as my secret shame was revealed. Vickers squinted at the clock, which had just ticked over to seven. He blinked and focused, saw me, and said, "Shall I bring you your usual whisky and soda, sir?"

ᕓ

"Let it go, Vickers. The burden of the secret was getting too much to carry, in any case. I feel liberated, like when that photograph appeared in *The Times* of me reading *Punch* during a performance of *La boheme*."

Vickers normally drifts off immediately the train leaves the station, but on this journey he was still aggrieved by his serendipitous slip of the tongue the night before. All was forgotten and forgiven and for the best, though, and now the sun was splitting the clouds and glimmering off the sea and dividing the rushing landscape on both sides of the train into uncountable shades of lush. An excellent day for a languorous, circuitous ricochet off Inverness to Edinburgh and points east through England.

Detective Sergeant Budge had dropped us off, along with a hundred-and-fifty-year-old case of Glen Glennegie, at the train station. I bought the case a ticket so that it could occupy the seat next to me and enjoy the scenery, and that's where it was now.

"We really ought to taste one of these while still on native soil, don't you think, Vickers?"

"That would be most appropriate, sir. I'll see if I can obtain two pony glasses from the dining car."

Vickers did just that while I opened a dusty bottle with a hand-written label that just said, I think, 'Glen Glennegie, 1755, aged five years'. When he came back he had two glasses and a sentimental box of salted almonds, which put us both in mind of someone else.

"Did I understand that Detective Sergeant Budge had sent a cable to Scotland Yard, asking them to intercept Miss Tannin on arrival in London?" asked Vickers in a distracted, whisky-pouring, box-opening manner.

"Yes. He did say that, I believe."

Vickers smiled that flat, paternal smile of the lifelong valet, who either shares the views of his employer in all things or smiles paternally when he does not. We raised our glasses and breathed our first scent of Glen Glennegie 1755.

"Promising," I announced.

"Most certainly," agreed Vickers.

Finally we tasted it raw and undiluted. The slightest sip asserted itself and seemed to physically grow and occupy all available taste receptors. It was a thousand layers of flavour and nuance, but in particular it was "Bluebells."

"Yes, sir."

"You sound unsurprised. Are you unsurprised, Vickers?"

"I noticed the subtlety when I first tasted it in 1909." Vickers closed his eyes to enjoy another slip of a sip.

"You knew about the bluebells?"

"Should I have mentioned it sooner?" asked Vickers.

"It would have made little difference, in the end," I assured him. "I have the Boisjolyan capacity for sounding like I know what I'm talking about, whether I do or not."

We travelled in silence but for the clackity tracks, steeped in green and rolling countryside and the wisp and echo of the waters and ways of Glen Glennegie. But something yet preoccupied Vickers.

"Will Miss Tibbits have gone to London?" Vickers spoke without judgement, but I could see it coming. "She struck me as a uniquely intelligent woman."

"No, Vickers, she won't have gone to London," I confessed. "There are a hundred places between here and there from which she can easily access a port and, from there, a rich network of contacts in Europe or America."

"I understand, sir."

"Do you, Vickers?"

Vickers replied with that Vickersian smile.

"It was the only way to give Budge a clean and conclusive resolution," I claimed.

Vickers' smile held.

"Very well, Vickers — while all that's true, I also very much did not want to be the one to send her to the gallows." I crunched an aloof almond and sipped a sullen whisky. "She's probably already in Bordeaux, or on a steamer to New York, but I expect she'll be caught sooner or later. I doubt very much she'll be exploding any more master distillers in the meantime, at any rate."

"I understand, sir," said Vickers once more, and then instantly fell asleep.

We had left the sea behind us and were now solidly in the untouched variety of the Highlands, in turns rough and rocky, smooth and streamy, pastoral and sheepy. In an instant, the generously sunny cinema of it all went dark in that screeching, sudden way of a fast train going through a tunnel. It was only a moment, but a sixth sense for Scotch told me that some disaster had struck, even before the lights came back on and I saw that one of the bottles of one-hundred-and-fifty-year-old Glen Glennegie was missing, and so were all the salted almonds.

Anty Boisjoly Mysteries

Thank you for reading this sixth Anty Boisjoly locked-room puzzler. I hope that you enjoyed *The Case of the Case of Kilcladdich* and I hope the solution wasn't too obvious and, simultaneously, not too deeply buried beneath all the secrets and subterfuge.

Anty Boisjoly mysteries are, clearly, not your typical manor-house murders, although I always try to include at least two impossible offings, an eccentric rogue's gallery of suspects, and a cosy setting. It's Anty's particular perspective and irrepressible good-humour, I think, that carve out a unique niche that I'm very, very grateful so many readers seem to appreciate.

If that includes you and you enjoy Anty Boisjoly and you know anyone like you, I hope you'll tell them about this series. If they're not like you, why not tell them anyway? It might give them some insights into how your mind works.

The Case of the Canterfell Codicil

The first Anty Boisjoly mystery

In *The Case of the Canterfell Codicil,* Wodehousian gadabout and clubman Anty Boisjoly takes on his first case when his old Oxford chum and coxswain is facing the gallows, accused of the murder of his wealthy uncle. Not one but two locked-room mysteries later, Boisjoly's pitting his wits and witticisms against a subversive butler, a senile footman, a single-minded detective-inspector, an irascible goat, and the eccentric conventions of the pastoral Sussex countryside to untangle a multi-layered mystery of secret bequests, ancient writs, love triangles, revenge, and a teasing twist in the final paragraph.

The Case of the Ghost
of Christmas Morning

The one you just read

In The Case of the Ghost of Christmas Morning, clubman, flaneur, idler and sleuth Anty Boisjoly pits his sardonic wits against another pair of impossible murders. This time, Anty Boisjoly's Aunty Boisjoly is the only possible suspect when a murder victim stands his old friends a farewell drink at the local, hours after being murdered.

The Tale of the Tenpenny Tontine

The dual duel dilemma

It's another mystifying, manor house murder for bon-vivant and problem-solver Anty Boisjoly, when his clubmate asks him to determine who died first after a duel is fought in a locked room. The untold riches of the Tenpenny Tontine are in the balance, but the stakes only get higher when Anty determines that, duel or not, this was a case of murder.

The Case of the Carnaby Castle Curse

The scary one

The ancient curse of Carnaby Castle has begun taking victims again — either that, or someone's very cleverly done away with the new young bride of the philandering family patriarch, and the chief suspect is none other than Carnaby, London's finest club steward.

Anty Boisjoly's wits and witticisms are tested to their frozen limit as he sifts the superstitions, suspicions, and age-old schisms of the mediaeval Peak District village of Hoy to sort out how it was done before the curse can claim Carnaby himself.

Reckoning at the Riviera Royale

The one with Anty's mum
Anty finally has that awkward 'did you murder my father' conversation with his mother while finding himself in the ticklish position of defending her and an innocent elephant against charges of impossible murder.

The Case of the Case of Kilcladdich

The source and origins of Anty's favourite tipple and pastime
Anty Boisjoly travels to the timeless source waters of Glen Glennegie to help decide the fate of his favourite whisky, but an impossible locked room murder is only one of a multitude of mysteries that try Anty's wits and witticisms to their northern limit.

Time trickles down on the traditional tipple as Anty unravels family feuds, ruptured romance, shepherdless sheep, and a series of suspiciously surfacing secrets to sort out who killed whom and how and why and who might be next to die.

The Foreboding Foretelling of Ficklehouse Felling

A manor-house classic expected mid-'23
It's a classic, manor house, mystery-within-a-locked-room-mystery for Anty Boisjoly, when a death is foretold by a mystic that Anty's sure is a charlatan. But when an impossible murder follows the foretelling, Anty and his old ally and nemesis Inspector Wittersham must sift the connivance, contrivance, misguidance, and reliance on pseudoscience of the household and its haunted history before the killer strikes again.

The Next Anty Boisjoly Mystery

We're always in constant danger of a new Anty Boisjoly mystery. If you'd like to be warned in advance you can sign up for the Consistently Infrequent Anty Boisjoly Newsletter...

https://indefensiblepublishing.com/books/pj-fitzsimmons/

Made in the USA
Columbia, SC
18 May 2023

16956059R00109